"Kiss me, Jordan," Ivy whispered.

Without hesitation, Jordan pulled her into his embrace and unleashed a passion so complete she was breathless within seconds. Ivy hugged him back, groping hungrily at his sweater. The kiss was frantic, urgent even. They ravished each other.

"I've been wanting to kiss you again since the day you left my room in New York," Ivy panted.

"And not one day has gone by without me thinking about kissing you again," Jordan admitted gruffly.

Ivy pulled him in for more. They kissed and kissed and kissed until both their bodies were on fire. Jordan's hands roamed Ivy's body and she explored all of his. Jordan's skin felt feverish under Ivy's touch.

Soon she wouldn't be able to control her cravings. She had to make a decision. Either send him home or take him to her bedroom.

* * *

Work-Love Balance by Nicki Night is part of the Blackwells of New York series.

NICKI NIGHT

———

WORK-LOVE BALANCE

HARLEQUIN

DESIRE

HARLEQUIN®
DESIRE™

Recycling programs for this product may not exist in your area.

ISBN-13: 978-1-335-58153-2

Work-Love Balance

Copyright © 2022 by Renee Daniel Flagler

For questions and comments about the quality of this book, please contact us at CustomerService@Harlequin.com.

Harlequin Enterprises ULC
22 Adelaide St. West, 41st Floor
Toronto, Ontario M5H 4E3, Canada
www.Harlequin.com

Printed in U.S.A.

A born and bred New Yorker, **Nicki Night** delights in creating hometown heroes and heroines with an edge. As an avid reader and champion of love, Nicki chose to pen romance novels because she believes that love should be highlighted in this world, and she delights in writing contemporary romances with unforgettable characters and just enough drama to make readers clutch a pearl here and there. Nicki has a penchant for adventure and is currently working on penning her next romantic escapade.

Books by Nicki Night

Harlequin Desire

Blackwells of New York

Intimate Negotiations
One More Second Chance
Work-Love Balance

Harlequin Kimani Romance

Her Chance at Love
His Love Lesson
Riding into Love

Visit her Author Profile page at Harlequin.com, or nickinight.com, for more titles.

You can also find Nicki Night on Facebook, along with other Harlequin Desire authors, at Facebook.com/harlequindesireauthors!

One

The Money Maven. That's what they called her now. Ivy Blackwell was still trying the moniker on for size. Sometimes she loved it. Other times it felt pretentious. Both times, it still made sense to her.

What didn't make sense was how fast the persona took off. It was startling, propelling her into the life of a social media influencer within one short year. And, with that, came the deals. Big deals. Of course, the Blackwell name had an impact but the hard work that it took keeping up with the demands of this lifestyle was all on Ivy. This was all new to her. It was exhilarating… yet it was also exhausting.

Ivy twirled, checking out her reflection in the mirrored wall in her walk-in closet. The black strapless gown couldn't have fit more perfectly. The large ruffle that ran down the side from her breast to the hem of her gown was almost obnoxious. It was way more flamboyant than she would have ever chosen for herself but she knew it was absolutely stunning and would certainly get lots of attention on the red carpet.

The thought of being in the spotlight made her a bit nervous. It's not like it was her first time. Her cousins were in the entertainment business. They practically ran Hollywood, producing shows and marrying A-listers. She'd gone to plenty of star-studded events with them but was always in the background. She wasn't an attention hog. In fact, too much attention made her uncomfortable. However, tonight, she wasn't going to be in the background. This was work. It was her job to be seen.

Ivy had been styled by an up-and-coming designer. This young woman hit the fashion scene with a vengeance, commanding the attention of popular celebrities. When the network invited Ivy to the launch party for *The Real Deal*, a reality show featuring female venture capitalists negotiating high-stakes business deals, this designer reached out and asked if she could style her for the big event. Ivy did her research on the young woman, fell in love with her work and responded with a "Hell, yeah!"

Jade, the makeup artist she hired for the evening, walked up to Ivy and dabbed her face with one of those fancy sponges.

"Take this with you so you can freshen up throughout the evening." She put a tube of lipstick in a small pouch and handed it to Ivy. "I also put a sponge in there so you can dab away the shine if you need to."

"Thanks, Jade." Ivy took a deep breath.

"Still nervous?" the woman asked.

"A little. This is—" she tried to find the right words "—just a lot. Look at me—a face full of makeup. This dress." Ivy ran her hand down the front of her body as if she were presenting herself. "This is way more than what I usually do. Actually, this is more my mother's speed."

"Girl! You're a Blackwell. You should be used to this."

"Don't get me wrong, I like to look fabulous just like any other gal, but this is different. This is my cousins' lifestyle. I never envied them for always being in the spotlight. We have our flashy few, but generally, people in finance are nothing like the entertainment industry."

"You've got a point," Jade said, sliding her brushes into the holder. "It *is* different. But you're made for this."

Ivy tilted her head. "You think so?"

"Of course." Jade stopped putting her makeup tools away and placed one hand on her hip. "You're the most stylish person I know in finance. Most of those women are ultraconservative in their suits and sheath dresses with their smart-looking selves. That's why you became popular so fast. You've got financial savvy, and pizzazz. With your chic style, you make learning about money seem cool. Smart and savvy is the new sexy, honey. That's why you're the Money Maven. You're the full package."

"Aww. Thanks."

"Seriously. Own it! Enjoy it. Think of times like these as a girl playing dress-up. Doesn't everyone like to play dress-up every now and then?" Jade asked as if the idea of not doing so was ridiculous.

Ivy twisted her lips thoughtfully. "I like that." She looked at herself in the mirror one more time, spun around and walked off like she'd just hit the runway. After a few steps, she took a dramatic pivot, tossed her hair over her shoulders and shot Jade a smoldering gaze as if she were posing on the red carpet.

"That's what I'm talking about!" The makeup artist threw her head back and laughed.

Ivy laughed with her.

"Ivy!" A male's baritone voice carried itself up her stairs.

"Ty!" She lifted her dress and shuffled as fast as she could. The gown hugged her legs. "Coming!"

Ivy made her way down the stairs swiftly and carefully, stepping into Tyson's waiting arms at the bottom. "What's up, cousin?"

He kissed her cheek, then held her at arm's length. With an approving smile, he took her in from head to toe. "Wow. You look stunning."

With a hand placed gently over her heart, Ivy said, "Thank you." She looked around. "Where's Kendall?" she asked as Jade made her way down the steps with her makeup kit the size of a carry-on bag.

Jade halted on the bottom step. "Wait! Tyson Blackwell is your cousin?"

"Yes, this big head is my cousin." Ivy swatted him on the back of his head, then nestled into his arm.

"Whoa!" Jade's eyes stretched wide. "I didn't even put that together. How cool!" She turned her attention to Tyson. "Pleasure to meet you. You're married to Kendall Chandler, right?"

"Yes, that's my lady."

"I love her music." Jade turned back to Ivy. "Have

a great night and remember what I told you. Call me when you come back to LA."

"I will." Ivy gave her an air kiss on both sides.

As Jade was walking out, Kendall came in the door. Jade stopped abruptly and just stared at Ty's wife. A second later, everyone laughed. They were used to that happening when Kendall was around.

"Hi!" Kendall held out her hand to Jade.

"Oh…um…my goodness. Kendall Chandler." Jade grabbed her hand and shook it hard. "This is so cool. It's a pleasure to meet you." Jade was still shaking Kendall's hand. "I'd love to do your makeup one day."

Kendall looked down at her hand still in Jade's grasp, then looked back up at Jade.

"Oh." Jade dropped Kendall's hand and nervously rubbed her hands along the sides of her legs. "Sorry."

Kendall laughed. "No problem. I'll get your information from Ivy."

"Wow! Okay. I should go. Wow. Um. Thanks. Have a great night, you all." Jade stepped through the door. When it closed behind her, Ivy heard her squeal. The three of them laughed again.

Kendall shook her head. "I don't know if I'll ever truly get used to that."

"I'm going to tell you like Jade just told me. *Own it!*" Ivy and Kendall laughed together. "Thanks for agreeing to join me tonight. They told me I could bring a plus one, but when I told them Tyson would be joining me, they said, 'And Kendall Chandler too, of course.' I told them you absolutely would. I'm just glad you were available so I wouldn't seem like a liar."

Tyson looked at his watch and said, "Time to go."

Ivy sucked in a heaping breath and let it out with a rush. "Well…" She held up her hands and let them fall to her sides. "Let's go."

The three headed out to the car. Their driver held the doors open until they were safely inside.

The next hour went by in a blur. Within minutes, they were on the red carpet. The popping sounds of camera flashes sparked in the air. Journalists, bloggers and entertainment commentators from every kind of media outlet captured the guests. Some held cameras with long fancy lenses, others had cell phones and everything in between.

"That's the Money Maven! Hey, Money Maven!" Ivy heard someone call out to her, but she could hardly see from all the flashing cameras.

Ivy smiled and posed. Pop, pop, pop went the cameras.

"Thank you!" one of the journalists yelled.

Ivy grinned again, waved and continued toward the door. She was surprised that person had noticed her. Because, truth be told, she wasn't sure how popular influencers were in the world of entertainment. She looked back to see that Tyson and Kendall were moving slowly down the carpet, posing and answering questions. They seemed so at ease to Ivy. She was still blinking from all the flashing lights.

Inside, they were ushered to a reception area. Waiters carried trays of wine and hors d'oeuvres. Ivy took a flute and sipped. Someone bumped her hard, causing the champagne to spill over the rim. She jumped back just in time to avoid splashing the liquid all over her dress.

Annoyed, Ivy turned toward the culprit holding her elbow to help steady her. She looked up into his face and the sharp words on the tip of her tongue stayed put as she snatched her arm from his grasp. She'd been ready to lash out but his drop-dead gorgeous looks had rendered her momentarily speechless. Besides, she also remembered that she was there on assignment. She couldn't cause a scene. Ivy was being paid the big bucks to appear at this event. Her job was to shoot short videos and take tons of pictures so she could chat it up on social media and influence people to want to download the network's app and watch the show when it aired. Cameras were everywhere. With all that in mind, she shoved her spicy response down her throat and nodded stiffly at his apology.

"I'm so sorry. I was in a rush and didn't see you. Did it get on your dress?" He looked down at her gown and she felt heat rise on her legs.

Ivy huffed. She remembered that this man had almost ruined her dress. "No!" she said sharply. She couldn't help the eye roll.

"Thank goodness. Again, my apologies."

Ivy only responded with a glare. She didn't trust her words. It didn't matter how handsome and poised this man was. She still felt the spot on the back of her shoulder where he'd bumped her, knocking her off balance. Had he been running?

After a few awkward seconds he bid her a good night, apologized one final time and walked off. Ivy couldn't help but watch him stride away. His swift gait was mesmerizing. She couldn't see under his tux, but something about his back let her know that it was strong and sturdy. His posture was regal. His pace purposeful. It was obvious that he had somewhere to be. He wasn't lingering, sipping champagne, greeting guests with a plastered smile while he nibbled bites like everyone else. Ivy watched him until he disappeared behind a set of double doors.

"You okay?"

Ivy was startled by Tyson's voice.

"Oh. Yeah. I'm fine."

"Ms. Blackwell?" A lean gentleman with a camera in one hand and cell phone in another stepped up to her. Ivy nodded. "I'm Dillon from the agency. I'll be working with you tonight to capture footage." His tone made his comment sound more like a question.

"Hello, Dillon. It's good to meet you."

"Likewise. All you need to do is interact and enjoy yourself. I'll capture as much footage as possible. Let us know how you feel, and how much you're enjoying the event. Okay?"

Ivy took a deep breath. "Okay."

"You'll be fine, Ms. Blackwell."

"Thank you, and please, call me Ivy."

"Okay. Let's get started."

Ivy sipped the remainder of the champagne in her glass and exhaled. She turned to Tyson and Kendall. "Might as well start with this fabulous couple." She stepped between her cousins so Dillon could snap several shots with a camera and then with his cell phone.

It took another glass of champagne for Ivy to get used to the fact that Dillon was following her around. But after a while, she felt herself loosening up and finally started to enjoy herself. Taking pictures with celebrities, the ladies from the show and then sitting down to watch the first episode of the new season were the highlights of her night. After the viewing, they were ushered into a ballroom to partake in the after-party.

Several times, she caught the guy who made her spill her drink looking at her. She ignored him, yet watched him discreetly in return. He'd interacted with Tyson at one point. They seemed quite familiar with one another. She refused to ask Tyson who he was. She wasn't there to meet men. Though she pretended to not see him, she couldn't get him off her mind.

Two

"We need something fresh," Jordan Chambers said, sitting back in the chair at the head of the executive boardroom and rubbing his chin. He knew the pressure was on. The competition in the television industry was fierce, forcing his production company to constantly keep good content in their pipeline. Some of the best options had recently been snatched up by other production companies and networks. "Our current shows are doing well, but at the same time, we need something new, different and binge worthy."

"You know Hollywood loves more of the same, but you're absolutely right," Anderson Parks, Jordan's vice president of programming, said. He stood and paced the glass conference room. "I know some networks are looking at the publishing industry for book-to-film options. There are a few authors that I've been watching…"

"That's good. Let's consider that, but we could use another reality smash hit," Jordan told Anderson. The others on his small team sat around the white marble table as well, looking pensive as they thought.

After a while, Jordan spoke up. "Let's take a look at the book lists."

"Don't forget social media. Flix TV just signed an influencer and her show has really taken off."

Jordan stood, walked to the whiteboard and made four columns: books, reality, dramas, influencers. "Okay," he said, turning back to his programming team of five. "Let's throw some ideas on the wall."

The crew called out suggestions for each category.

"I have some friends in the big six," Jordan said, referring to the largest publishing houses. "I can check what books are on the schedule to drop in the next few months and we can see if there's something there. We can do some more book-to-film deals."

"What about that money woman?" Anderson asked. "She's an influencer that talks about finances, investing and all that. I just read an article about her. They call her the Money Maven. She's got a book coming out soon. Not to mention, she's hot!" Anderson picked up his cell phone and thumbed through it. "This is her," he said, turning his phone so his team members could see. "She's got over a million followers now. We can do a reality show with her."

"Let me see that." Jordan took the VP's phone and looked through her profile. He tilted his head.

There was something familiar about her. Then he

realized where he'd seen her. It was the same woman he'd bumped into at *The Real Deal* event. Immediately he remembered the fire in her eyes when he made her spill her drink. Luckily her dress wasn't ruined. Jordan also remembered how beautiful she was…

"You know her?" Anderson asked, bringing Jordan's attention back to the present.

"No. I ran into her at the event the other night." He paused there and handed the phone back to Anderson. Jordan remembered what she was like based on the way she glared at him. Despite being in Hollywood, huge egos were a turnoff. He'd dealt with them because it was part of his world but he didn't always like it.

Furrowing his brow, Jordan recalled more about that event. He'd taken her in a few times that evening despite being busy. He was there to rub elbows for a few upcoming deals. But something about her pulled him in throughout the night. He kept finding her. Each time, he'd watch her for a moment, mindful not to stare too long. Once or twice, she caught him, but her expression seemed blank. He couldn't tell what she was thinking. Jordan figured she was annoyed about the near miss with her dress. "Women," he'd whispered to himself and left it alone.

"You know what?" Something came to Jordan's mind at that very moment. "I think I remember seeing her with Tyler Blackwell."

"Actually, I think they might be related," Anderson said. "Look." He walked his phone over to Jordan and scrolled through her profile. "She was there on business. Look at all these posts about the event." Anderson squinted as he read through a short bio on her Instagram profile. "Her name is Ivy Blackwell. And she has a bunch of pictures with Tyler and his wife, Kendall Chandler."

"Let's see if she has something in the works with Tyler's media company," another programming team member said.

"Possibly, but BMG is into movies and dramatic series. They don't really touch reality," Jordan mused. "Let's put her on the list," he announced.

He spun on his heels and wrote Tyler's name on the board next to hers in parentheses.

"Good call," Anderson said. "And I'll do some research on her new book and find out who's on her team."

"Perfect." Jordan smiled. Despite their inauspicious start, he wouldn't mind working with the woman. It looked like her social media following could be a win for their company. And he couldn't help but acknowledge how stunning she was. Jordan just hoped that his first impression of her was wrong. She didn't seem very nice and the last thing he needed was one more entitled, egotistical, celebrity brat to deal with. "Let's get some more names on this board."

Jordan's phone rang. When his mother's number flashed across his phone, he paused, wondering if he should answer, send her to voice mail or shoot her a text letting her know he'd call her right back. Charisse Lane didn't often call during business hours.

"Excuse me." He put up a finger dismissing himself and stepped out of the conference room as he answered. "How's my favorite lady?"

"Hey, sweetie. Your mama's...fine."

Jordan noticed the hesitation. He looked toward his

team still brainstorming and walked farther down the hall to avoid being heard. "Everything okay, Mom?"

"Well. Not exactly…"

Jordan's heart leaped in his chest. "What's wrong? What do you need?"

"Well…" After another pregnant pause Charisse continued. "It's Timothy."

Jordan let out the breath he'd been holding. His mother was okay, but her husband, Timothy, was a different situation. He remained cordial with his stepfather for his mother's sake. "What's wrong with him?" Jordan's words came out sharper than he'd intended.

"He needs a little help."

"With all due respect, Mom, you're calling me to help that man?"

"Honey. I know how you feel about Timmy, but this impacts both of us."

Jordan huffed. He wanted to immediately say no to whatever it was but this was his mother asking and he had to hear her out. There wasn't anything he wouldn't do for her.

"Can you call us right after work, please?"

"What's…" Jordan stopped himself from asking what this was all about. It didn't matter. He wasn't going to like it.

"Please, Jordan," his mother pleaded after his abrupt pause.

Several more beats of silence passed. "Okay. I'll call at five thirty. Okay?" That would give him time to get to his condo and it wouldn't be too late for his mom, considering the three-hour time difference between LA and New York.

"That's perfect. Thank you, sweetie."

"See you later, Mom." He wanted to say more but decided to leave it for now.

After ending the call, he paced a bit before going back into the conference room. He needed to get his mind in check. What did his stepfather want with him? They hadn't been on good terms since he'd married his mother when he and his brother, Dorian, were teens. In fact, he was the reason that Jordan and Dorian vowed not to return home after college. They refused to continue living with that man. Yet, somehow, he seemed to make their mother's life better at a time where she was at her lowest. Despite their feelings for Timothy, seeing their mother happy made it easier for them to tolerate their stepfather's existence. They worked hard to be cordial to the man for Charisse's sake.

Jordan took a deep breath, held it in for a moment and let it out slowly before heading back into the conference room. He'd spent the next fifteen minutes trying to concentrate on the meeting but couldn't stay focused.

"Let's pick this back up tomorrow. That will give us some time to come up with some more fresh ideas."

Anderson tilted his head and eyed Jordan. He sensed the questions behind the other man's eyes. Jordan may have been able to fool the rest of his team, but Anderson was a different story. They were close friends and had been working together too long for Anderson not to sense when something was off with Jordan.

"Sure. Let's leave all of that up for tomorrow," Anderson said, pointing to the board they used to post their ideas.

Jordan was the first to leave the conference room.

Anderson was on his heels but said nothing until they were behind closed doors in Jordan's palatial office. The glass walls overseeing Wilshire Boulevard flooded the space with natural light.

Jordan walked in past his desk and chair and looked out at the view. He watched the people mill about on the pavement below him. Anderson sat back on the navy tufted sofa and crossed one leg over the other. Neither spoke for several moments.

"My mother called," Jordan finally said.

"Is she okay?"

He shrugged. "She seems fine."

"Say no more. I just knew something was off."

"It's *him*."

Anderson sighed hard. Jordan heard his huff from behind but continued focusing on the movement down on Wilshire Boulevard. Anderson knew his history. He got how much he disliked his stepfather. And knew how much the man got under his skin.

"Is he okay?"

"Don't know yet." Jordan finally turned to face his friend. "I guess I'll find out tonight. My mom asked that I call later to talk. I don't know what it's about, but it can't be good."

Anderson shook his head and then stood. "Let me know if you need me, man."

"I'm sure Dorian will be there. I'll be fine."

Anderson tugged on the sleeves of his tailored button-down shirt. "Call me if you want to grab a drink after."

"Will do."

Anderson exited Jordan's office, and Jordan went back to looking out the window. He needed to prepare his mind for tonight. He was either going to need a drink or coffee before talking to his mother and stepfather. He opted for coffee before and a drink after.

Jordan put in a few more hours before leaving the office. He headed to his favorite coffee shop, owned by a friend. They had filmed a few scenes from different shows at this place. With his eyes lowered to the phone in his hand, he opened the door to the coffee shop and collided with a woman on her way out.

The cup gave, the lid tumbled off and the steaming hot beverage lifted into the air and came crashing down on both of them. It all seemed to happen in slow motion until he felt the heat from the liquid on his chest. The woman gasped and jumped back to avoid more of the coffee hitting her. She pulled at her blouse, moving it away from her skin. Jordan glanced over at her angry face and couldn't believe this was happening again.

"I'm so sorry, miss."

The woman looked back at him with wide eyes and huffed. Recognition set in for both of them at the same time. It was the same woman from the other night.

"You have to be kidding me," she said, glaring at him.

Jordan didn't know what was hotter, the coffee singeing his skin or the heat from her glare. He shook his head. "Man, I'm *really* sorry. Please. Let me help you." Jordan stepped past her and reached for napkins at the stand next to the door.

"No." The woman held both hands up. "No. Thank you! I don't want your help." Her words were harsh. She went back inside and headed for the bathroom.

Jordan pulled napkins from the dispenser, wiped his shirt and ordered an Americano for him and another of whatever it was that the woman was drinking. Though his friend, the owner, wasn't there, he waited a while for the woman to come out of the bathroom. When the barista handed her a fresh cup, she pointed in Jordan's direction. Jordan lifted his cup in acknowledgment. The woman took the cup from the barista, smiled tightly, turned toward Jordan and glared one last time before marching out of the coffee shop.

What were the chances of him spilling a drink on the same woman twice? Jordan hoped his day wouldn't get any worse.

Three

Ivy couldn't believe her luck. How did she have two drinks spilled on her by the same person in a matter of days? This time, there was no getting away. No matter how much scrubbing she did in the bathroom, she couldn't get the brown stains out of her white shirt. She'd definitely have to go back to her hotel room before meeting up with Tyler. She was exhausted. Adding another stop to her busy day was the last thing she wanted to do. Between the lack of sleep and today's crazy schedule, she wasn't sure how she would get through the next few hours.

She tapped out a text to her cousin to let him know she needed to push their dinner back a bit. Irritation had her fingers moving across her phone screen at lightning speed. After texting Tyler, she exited the bathroom, retrieved her replacement drink from the barista and only half nodded a sentiment of appreciation to the gentleman after the barista told her he'd paid for it. At least he'd bought her another drink. That was a decent enough gesture. She got an Uber and headed back to the hotel. Within an hour she entered the restaurant where Tyler and Kendall had been waiting for her.

"I'm so sorry I'm late," she said in rush as she flopped into the chair. "You won't believe what happened."

"It's fine." Kendall dismissed Ivy's concern with a wave of her hand. "We ordered for you. I know you need to get back to make your red-eye tonight. This good?" she asked, pointing to what she'd ordered for Ivy.

"Yep. That's perfect."

"Good. So, what happened?" Tyler prodded, bringing them back to what Ivy had just said.

Ivy told them about her second run-in with the man and her ruined shirt.

"Are you kidding me?" Kendall said. "What are the chances?"

Tyler shook his head.

"I know, right? If I didn't know better, I'd think that guy had it out for me," Ivy huffed.

"Well, in any event, I'm glad we get to see you once more before you head back home," Kendall said. "The next time you come back to LA, we won't be here."

"I know. Are you excited about the tour? How long will you be away?" Ivy asked as Tyler flagged down their waiter.

"Tyler and I will be in Scotland for a few weeks shooting the new movie. The tour starts after that. I'll have a short break between the US dates and the ones overseas."

"That album really took off. I'm proud of you. How do you do it all?" Ivy asked.

"I really take advantage of my downtime. After the tour, I'll have about two solid months of rest before having to do anything else."

"Yes. We plan to be off the grid for at least one of those months," Tyler said and kissed Kendall's forehead. "I'll have my wife all to myself."

"We're going to take a trip." Kendall sang the last word. Her face lit up with excitement. Then she turned to Tyler, flashed a tender smile and gently touched the back of his hand. Her husband winked at her.

"I've been promising to take her on an excursion. We're going to stay at the house in Montana for a few weeks and then head overseas."

"That's sweet," Ivy said, leaning her head sideways. "Two months off the grid is great, but until then, things are nonstop. Really...how do you do it?"

Ivy wasn't just being curious. She really wanted to know. This new life of hers had become so demanding. Several times in the past year, she entertained fleeting thoughts of walking away from it all.

Ivy thought starting and running that women's group at Blackwell the year before was a lot. There, she'd spent countless hours planning events, facilitating workshops and teaching women about finance and wealth building. These efforts extended her workday and filled up her calendar on the weekends. It was so empowering, and her father was ecstatic about the company's growth with the surge of female clients. But then, her popularity grew among women's organizations, which is what led to Ivy's current situation and the angst between her and her parents, Bill and Lydia.

One conference appearance led to Ivy becoming an influencer. That paved the way for the book deal and now she was completely exhausted all of the time. But Ivy wasn't a quitter.

After the waitress placed their orders on the table, Ivy asked Kendall one more time, "Please, help me with this. How do you do it all? I'm not doing half as much as you and I'm exhausted. This influencer life is not what I expected and I see no end in sight. I'm grateful for all the opportunities, but I don't know how long I will be able to keep this up *and* keep my job."

Kendall and Tyler looked at each other and then back at Ivy.

"Quit!" Kendall and Tyler both said that with such ease Ivy's heart sank.

But in all honesty, that thought had crossed her mind over the past few months as well. Her position at Blackwell made this life possible for her. Even though she was often drained, she really did enjoy reaching women all over the country and felt as though this was her way to give back to the world for all she'd been able to gain. She was proud of what she'd accomplished at Blackwell in a short period of time and becoming an influencer gave her the ability to increase her impact exponentially. Ivy also thought about how her parents would feel if she quit. Another Blackwell, walking away from everything they worked so hard to build for them. How would she even break that news to her father?

"Ivy!"

"Huh?" Ivy looked up at Kendall and Tyler, realizing she'd been lost in her thoughts. "I'm sorry."

"You don't want to walk away from the family business, do you?" Tyler asked.

Ivy sighed. "I don't."

"Is it that *you* don't want to walk away or you don't want to disappoint Uncle Bill and Aunt Lydia?"

Ivy's shoulder slumped and she groaned. "Both."

"How do they feel about everything you're doing outside of your work at Blackwell?"

Ivy frowned. "They're not impressed. They think I'm cheapening my image—i.e., the *Blackwell* image."

"Yeah," Tyler said. He and Kendall nodded knowingly.

"I get it, Ivy. My family is very similar to yours, but for your sanity, one day you'll be forced to choose. A lot can come out of this for you. In fact, a lot has. This new book deal, you've made a name for yourself."

"Yeah," Ivy said. "That's part of the problem according to Dad. I already had a name to be proud of. Mom said the Money Maven sounds like I run a brothel." She laughed. She'd gotten used to the jab but deep down it still stung.

"Want my advice?" Kendall asked.

"Yeah! That's what I've been asking for."

"Give yourself time to think about what you really want. You'll learn how to manage your demanding life just like we did. It's still new to you. Just remember to take the time you need to unplug and refresh yourself. Most importantly, every important decision you make for yourself has the potential to make someone unhappy. Who will it be? You or them?"

Kendall's last statement hit hard. Ivy had some thinking to do. Questions raced through her mind. Whose happiness would she have to sacrifice in order to have the life she wanted most? What did she really want? What was missing in her life? Could she make room for love?

Four

Jordan tried hard to concentrate but his mind kept wandering to last night's conversation with his mother and stepfather. He hadn't been able to get Dorian on the phone yet, which meant he'd been holding in all of his thoughts about his stepfather's request. When he finally got a text back from Dorian, his brother promised to call later that evening.

Anderson tapped on Jordan's office door before peeking in. "You're in early."

"Yeah." Jordan released a slow breath. "I wanted to get an early start. Couldn't sleep anyway, so I decided to come in." He glanced at his watch. "Why are you here so early?"

"One of my contacts came through big-time!" Anderson stepped all the way into Jordan's office and clasped his hands together. He smiled. "I think we picked a winner but of course we'll have to act fast. I wanted to get some stuff together in time for our meeting this morning so I can share my findings with everyone!"

"I could use some good news." Jordan waved Anderson all the way in and gestured toward the chair in front of his desk.

Anderson danced a two-step, shuffling his way toward Jordan's desk, and sat down. His smile widened. "Are you ready for this?"

"Yep. Spill it." Jordan learned forward, ready to take in whatever it was that his VP of programming had for him.

"As I said, my contact at the publishing house came through big-time. They're dropping a book by the Money Maven in a couple of weeks. Ivy Blackwell's really hot right now. I told him we're looking for something new for the networks and how I thought maybe a reality show with her helping people get rich or fix money problems would be great! We could work together with the book launch—maybe even promote the launch as part of the promotion for the show. This book could hit the *New York Times* list and be a huge win for both of us." He cleared his throat. "He loved the idea—said he'll speak with his executive team today so they can hop on this ASAP since they have TV and film rights for the book. We can meet with them while we're in New York next week."

Jordan tilted his head. "I think she lives here. We should try to meet with her before we head to New York. See if you can get her contact information."

"I'm on it!"

Jordan loved the idea. It was timely and he knew it could work. They needed fresh content to present to the networks. Jordan wondered how well that Ivy Blackwell woman would take to an offer from his company. Surely a little spilled wine and coffee wouldn't be enough for her to walk away from a great deal. If Jordan was completely honest, he'd admit that he really wanted to see Ivy again. He could still feel the remnants of the spark he felt when his body touched hers. Her eyes, though they sparkled with a bit of feistiness, still drew him in.

Anderson shot up from his seat, promising to reach out to her publisher, and Jordan gave him a thumbs-up before the other man headed out. This new development energized him and made him forget about his family situation for a moment. When thoughts of the previous evening came back, Jordan brushed them away and tried to focus.

Excited about the prospect of the new show, Jordan jotted down a few ideas for a pilot. Then he picked up his cell phone and searched through the Money Maven's social media profiles. From his unfortunate and limited interaction with the woman, he didn't know much about her. He knew social media only told half the story but he wanted to find out as much about her as possible. She came from a family of finance kings and queens in New York. Hailing from New York with most of his family still residing there, he knew that her family affiliation alone spoke volumes. He'd seen Tyler Blackwell with her at the event. Now he understood their connection. They were cousins.

Ivy's online presence was well curated and polished. It exuded wealth and luxury, yet she still managed to come across as professional and down to earth. She had short videos offering financial tips that also showed her sense of humor. He could see why her followers loved her. They wanted to be like her.

Jordan found what he'd been looking for, but continued scrolling through her profiles. The more he discovered about Ivy, the more he liked the idea of working with her. With competition in the industry becoming stiffer by the day, he needed to keep his pipeline of new show ideas full. His team had never worked harder.

Jordan scrolled across pictures from the event. She was just as beautiful as he remembered. One thing he did notice was that she didn't seem to have a significant other in her life. Perhaps she kept her personal business on a separate profile.

Jordan came across one private account and assumed it had to be her but couldn't tell by the profile picture because she wasn't showing her full face. This made him even more curious about her. What was she like behind her public facade? He was intrigued by the fact that there wasn't much personal information about her on social media.

Jordan's last girlfriend, Mya, was a social media fiend, constantly posting pictures, checking her DMs and inbox messages and looking for new comments and likes on her posts. He was always in competition with her phone when it came to getting her attention. They couldn't even go out for dinner without her taking tons of pictures to post throughout the evening. She ate up the attention she received from her fans. It was all too much for a humble guy like Jordan.

Sadly, they'd reached an impasse in their relationship. She complained about the long hours he put into his production company and he complained about how much time she spent focusing on her social media. One day he came home to the sprawling house they shared and found it empty. He knew they'd had their problems, but he'd loved her and considered her the one that got away. Eventually, he blocked her on social media. He couldn't bear to see her constant posts and yet have no access to her. She belonged to her friends and followers, not to him anymore.

Almost a year later, he ran into her and was shocked to see an engagement ring and her swollen belly. A pang shot through his heart. Their brief, awkward encounter gave him closure. She'd run from his house straight into the arms of another man. Jordan wondered if he was around while they were still together.

Looking at his watch, Jordan realized more than a half hour had passed. He put the phone down and turned his attention to his laptop. He continued doing research on Ivy Blackwell online. Pictures of her with a microphone in her hand came up. He read about the successful women's initiative she launched at Blackwell. Several interviews gave him the chance to hear her voice. This woman was brilliant. He got new ideas about a show after checking her out. Her voice was full and mellow like that of a jazz singer. Jordan could listen to her all day.

After switching his focus to other business matters, his stepfather's request came back to mind again. Jordan reached for the phone again. He dialed Dorian's number. His brother didn't answer but he sent a text saying he'd call him later that evening. Jordan huffed.

His phone rang a half hour later. He reached for it quickly, hoping it was Dorian calling earlier than he'd mentioned. It was his mother.

"Hey, Mom." He tried not to sound like all the cheer had been siphoned from his tone.

"I was checking on you."

"I'm fine, Ma. How about you?"

"I'm good. I just wanted you to know that I appreciate you hearing your stepfather out last night."

Jordan held his breath a moment before answering. "Sure. You're welcome."

"I was thinking, honey. It's been a while since I've seen you. When are you coming home for a visit?"

"Me and my team are actually planning to be in NYC for a few meetings next week."

"Oh, great!" His mother's voice rose, her enthusiasm evident. "When are you coming in?"

"I was planning on arriving Sunday but I can come a day earlier."

"That would be great! We can do brunch on Sunday."

"I'd be happy to take my favorite lady to brunch." Jordan hoped she wouldn't ask for that husband of hers to join them.

"Great, honey. It will be my treat."

"Not on my watch, Ma. I'll pick you up at noon on Sunday."

"That would be perfect. I can't wait to see you."

"I can't wait to see you either." Jordan felt a smile spread across his face. After more small talk, he said goodbye to his mother.

Putting his phone down, he thought about the day Tim Lane came into their lives. It was two years after they'd lost their father. Jordan, Dorian and his mother were buried in grief. Tim seemed like a knight in shining armor and Jordan was sure he would fill the gaping void that their father's sudden death had left. That didn't happen. Tim doted on their mom, but Jordan and Dorian seemed nothing more than a burden to him. They were in Tim's way. Now this man wanted his help.

Five

"Wait! *What?*" Ivy stood abruptly, almost knocking over her office chair. Her mouth dropped open. "A television show!" Ivy ran to close her office door. She didn't want anyone to hear this. "Oh, my goodness." She covered her gaping mouth.

"Yes!" her agent, Jamie, said. "This. Is. Huge."

"Wow!" Slowly, Ivy sat down on the white couch inside her office. She took a deep breath. "I never imagined."

"Well, it's happening. The producers will be in town next week. They want to meet with you."

"What day?" A short wave of anxiety squiggled through Ivy's stomach. Her schedule was already booked solid but she had to make time for this. Ivy thought about how limited her time was already. She couldn't say no to a TV show, but how could she possibly fit filming a show into her schedule too?

"Tuesday at ten thirty. Will that work?" Jamie asked, breaking into Ivy's thoughts,

"Um…hold on." She flipped thorough the calendar on her phone. "Unfortunately, I have a meeting at that time."

"Oh, man," Jamie said. "They need to meet with us before their meeting with the network. I don't think we have another option. Is there anything you can do? Meanwhile I can try to see if another time would be possible."

Ivy rubbed her temple. "Okay. Please ask. If they can't meet any other time, then book it. I'll work things out on my side."

"Good. I'll get all of the details to you and meet you there."

"Wow! My own show," Ivy whispered.

"Yep. Your very own show. I'll call you back when I have some updates."

"Thanks, Jamie. Bye."

When the call ended, Ivy sat on the couch staring at nothing in particular. She was shocked. Being an influencer had garnered so much attention and time. It was starting to challenge her ability to continue her work at Blackwell. Speaking of Blackwell, Ivy's meeting on Tuesday was with Dale Billington, an heiress to a huge portfolio of businesses and real estate in New York. If she landed this account, Dale would be the largest client Ivy ever secured. It took months to pin her down. Dale was extremely particular and didn't want to meet with anyone else besides Ivy after seeing her in an article.

Ivy flopped back on the couch. Again, her influencer life was running interference with work. She'd promised her dad, Bill, that it wouldn't. She'd sold him on this idea of Blackwell Wealth needing a woman in a high-profile position to bring in more females. It worked. She told her idea to her brother's wife, Zoe. She also loved the idea and agreed to come back to Blackwell to help Ivy run the women's division. With Ivy in the lead, she and Zoe attracted an impressive clientele of wealthy women, growing the company's visibility and customer base exponentially. Ivy was proud of their accomplishments, but increasingly, her burgeoning fame had caused conflict both within the company and her family.

Ivy dialed Zoe.

When Zoe answered she stood and started pacing again.

"Uh…you're calling me from down the hall?"

"I need you to come to my office right this moment." Ivy spoke slowly and steadily, making every effort to control the tone of her voice. But deep down she felt like screaming.

Moments later, Zoe poked her head in. She looked at Ivy pacing and stepped into the office cautiously. Her eyes on Ivy and full of questions. "Okay, sister. Spill it!"

"Come!" Ivy grabbed her sister in-law's hand and dragged her to the couch. "Sit." Ivy sat and pulled Zoe down next to her."

"What's going on?" the other woman asked.

"I was offered a television show!"

"What?" Zoe shrieked.

Ivy covered Zoe's mouth. "Shhh!" She looked at her

office door before continuing. Ivy got up and led Zoe to the chair in front of her desk. Zoe's hand was still over her opened mouth.

"A television show?" Zoe whispered.

Ivy laughed. She wasn't ready for Zoe to tell the world but she didn't have to whisper. "Yes. I can't believe it." Ivy put her hand on her heart and walked over to the windowed wall. She looked down at the traffic rushing along Sixth Avenue. The people looked miniscule. She turned back to Zoe.

"Well!" Zoe said impatiently. "Tell me all about it!"

Ivy trotted over and sat on the edge of her desk facing the other woman. "This is all I know." She told Zoe about her conversation with Jamie and the conflict with the meeting times.

"Oh, no!" Zoe sat back, sucked in a deep breath and released it slowly. "We have to figure something out. It took forever to get this appointment with Dale." She stood up and paced Ivy's office. "I'm assuming you haven't spoken to Pop yet?" That's what Zoe called Mr. Blackwell.

"Of course not! I need to sort everything out first. I know rescheduling with Dale is not an option, so I'm hoping Jamie can get the time switched of this meeting with these producers."

"Oh, my goodness, Ivy!" Zoe lifted her eyes to the ceiling and shook her head. She laughed. "A freaking television show. Unbelievable! How are you going to keep up with everything?"

"I have no idea but this is too good to pass up. As a kid I used to imagine myself doing talk shows like *The View*. I saw myself sitting at a table with a few fabulous women talking about all kinds of topics, interviewing celebrities. That aspiration faded away when I went for my MBA and ended up working for Dad. So, yeah, this is like a dream come true. I would never have imagined."

Zoe crossed her arms and shook her head.

"And!" Ivy raised a finger at Zoe. "We have to keep this to ourselves. You have to promise."

"He won't—"

"Zoe!" Ivy scolded. "Promise me you won't say anything to Ethan. I can't have this get back to Dad until I know for sure what's going to happen."

"Fine." Zoe dropped her shoulders. "I promise."

Ivy stared at her, doubting she wasn't going to share this news with her husband, which was also Ivy's brother Ethan. The two were spouses and the best of friends. They kept nothing from each other.

"Okay. Stop looking at me like that. I won't say a thing. But as soon as it's okay to tell, you have to let me know," Zoe said. "Ethan is going to lose his mind."

"Ugh. You're a mess. I will."

"In the meantime—" Zoe headed for the door as she spoke "—we need to figure out how to make both meetings happen. Let me know as soon as you hear back from your agent."

"I will!" Ivy huffed. She had to make this work.

Her sister-in-law opened the door and stepped through. She turned back. "You're in town next week, right?"

"Yes. I have that awards dinner, remember?"

"Oh, yes! The Forty Under Forty Awards. So, you're definitely joining us for Ethan's birthday dinner Tuesday evening?"

"Sure will."

"And I'll be forced to keep this a secret the whole time."

"You sure will!" Ivy raised a brow.

Zoe raised her hand to her lips and pretended to turn a key. Then she whispered, "You're going to be a star!" She giggled her way out the door.

Ivy threw her head back and laughed, but that joy didn't last long. She dragged herself behind her desk and plopped into her chair. She looked at her reflection in the mirror that sat on her desk. Her eyes had bags under them. The light makeup did little to hide the weariness. How was she going to do it all? And what would this mean for her position at Blackwell?

Six

Up until the time Jordan picked up his mother from her house in Jamaica Estates, Queens, thoughts of Ivy Blackwell had been wandering through his mind. She would be perfect for the show he had in mind. He watched her zany Instagram reels revealing snippets of her personality and explored some of the sound financial advice she'd doled out across the internet. He even called his broker and snagged a couple hundred shares of a stock she'd added to her "ones to watch" after doing some research. He loved the fact that she was a strong advocate for community service and helped women build wealth. His mother could have used someone like her in her life after his father passed.

That said, her level of interaction on social media alarmed him just a bit, because of his previous girlfriend

Mya's obsession with it. How much of her online presence did she actually manage herself and how much was done by her team? More and more, he wanted to know the woman behind the public persona of the Money Maven.

A smile spread across his face as he pulled into his mother's driveway. Charisse had been waiting on his arrival. She came running out the front door with arms wide open. Jordan got out of the car and stepped right into her waiting embrace.

"Oh! My baby is home!" Charisse squeezed him tight. In turn, Jordan wrapped his arms around his mother and lifted her in the air.

"How are you, pretty lady?" He lowered her gently until her feet hit the ground.

"So much better now that my baby boy is here."

Jordan chuckled and rolled his eyes toward the sky.

Charisse reached up and placed her palm on his cheek. "I don't care how old you are, you're always going to be my baby boy." She stepped back from him, took both his hands in hers and looked up at him. With the inheritance of their father's height, he and Dorian towered over their mom. She came no higher than their strong pecs. "You're getting too skinny. We've got to find you nice lady. Not another tricky one that's going to run out on you."

"Ma!" Jordan scolded and laughed. To Charisse, every issue with him and Dorian lead back to them not having a "nice lady" in their lives. If they lost weight, or gained weight. If they came down with a head cold or pulled a muscle at the gym, it was because they needed a good woman. She took every chance she could to remind them about their bachelor status whether it made sense or not. It became a running joke in their family.

"Okay!" She waved him off before he could continue. "Let's go eat!" She walked back to the house to lock the door and climbed in the passenger side of the car. "They've got a great new place in Long Beach that's right on the water. I want to go there." Charisse reached over and tapped her way through the on-screen navigation and put in the address.

"Have you ever seen that…" His mother paused. Jordan cringed and held his breath. "That…woman…since that day?"

Jordan released the breath he'd been holding and laughed before pulling out of the driveway. He was sure she was going to come out with a more insulting word than *woman*. She'd done it several times before. It was obvious that Charisse was trying to be nicer about her inquiries, despite the fact that she was still clearly upset by Mya's abrupt departure.

"No, Ma. I haven't seen her since then."

"Does it still bother you, honey?"

"Not anymore."

"Good, because it still bothers me. Is that why you haven't started dating again yet?"

"Ma!"

"Well, have you at least met any nice women lately? No prospects?"

Jordan shook his head at this mother's insistence, but the image of Ivy in that beautiful gown at the wrap party popped into his mind. He felt that same magnetic feeling he had that night as he watched her. Even after he upset her with his clumsiness. What if? Jordan chided himself, rolling his eyes discreetly before chuckling quietly.

"Ma!" He laughed. "No prospects yet, okay?" Even as he said these words to his mother, he wondered about Ivy.

"Okay! I'll drop it. I just want you and your brother happy. That bachelor life will get you in big trouble these days. You two need to find yourselves a good woman and settle down. I keep telling y'all. I worry."

"Ma!" Jordan scolded her with his tone again. "There's nothing to worry about."

"Okay! Okay!" Charisse broke out in joyful laughter. "I'm just so glad to see you. You have to come home more often. Or stay longer when you do come. I miss you," she whined as she said those last words.

Charisse patted his arm and then snuggled into her seat. She chatted all the way to the restaurant, barely allowing Jordan to get a word in. In fact, his mom was so preoccupied with catching him up on everything that had happened since his last visit that she never noticed Dorian enter the restaurant until he was standing right next to their table.

"Oh!" Charisse shrieked and hopped to her feet. "You mean to tell me I get to spend time with *both* my babies today?" She wrapped her arms around Dorian, laying the side of her face against his chest.

"Hey, Ma!" Dorian hugged his mother back and kissed the top of her head.

"What a nice surprise. We'll need more mimosas!" She threw her hands in the air. All three laughed.

Dorian greeted his brother with a hug, took his seat at the table and ordered his meal. For a while they ate and simply enjoyed each other's company. But eventually they had to breech the subject of why Jordan invited Dorian to their brunch. Yes, they hadn't seen their mother in a while and were incredibly close to her, but neither of the boys made big business decisions without the other since both were heavily invested in each other's companies.

Dorian, though he didn't make it to the pros, was a staunch sports fan. His athletic physique was evidence that he'd kept up his workout regimen. After college he launched a company that manufactured a sports energy drink that garnered endorsements by many of his athlete friends who did make it to the pros. Over a year later, their support turned the drink into a billion-dollar brand.

After her meal, Charisse delicately wiped her mouth with her napkin and placed it on the table. She sat back and sighed. "That was delicious."

"It was," Dorian agreed. Jordan, still chewing, shook his head.

"Now let's get this out of the way before I have my dessert," the older woman said. She'd never been one to dance around important subjects. She was always ready and willing to face situations head-on. "Let me explain why we're asking for your help with Tim's business."

Jordan and Dorian shared a quick glance.

Charisse looked at Jordan and then Dorian before spreading her lips into a loving smile. "I know you're not fond of him. And you never seem to believe me when I say he really cares about you boys."

This time, Jordan and Dorian exchanged doubtful glances.

"I know you said you'll think about it and discuss it with each other, but I need you to not say no to him," Charisse said.

"Why?" Jordan said.

"Because the reason his business is in trouble is because of me. He would never come to you two to bail him out. Like you, he has too much pride. But he also wouldn't reveal the fact that I caused this issue."

Jordan looked at Charisse, waiting for more. Dorian's expression showed he was questioning what their mother could have possibly done as well.

Their mom's eyes suddenly looked sullen.

Dorian put down his fork. "What is it, Ma?"

Charisse heaved a huge sigh. "I had this idea to start a company. Tim has taken wonderful care of me all these years, but I felt like I needed something for myself."

"What kind of company?" Dorian asked.

Charisse shrugged. "A trucking business."

Both Dorian's and Jordan's brows furrowed, and they looked at one another and then back at their mother.

"A *trucking* business?" Jordan asked. Though that seemed odd, Jordan had always credited their mother for passing down her entrepreneurial spirit to them. Charisse had always found ways to reinvent herself.

"I can't wait to hear this," Dorian said dryly.

"I wanted to do something different. Bold. We used some of our savings and Tim took money from his company to invest in the business. We got a small fleet of trucks, set up our offices, hired drivers and got things going. I loved it, but shortly after, Tim was diagnosed with prostate cancer." She blew out a breath. "The doctor said if we treated it aggressively, we could get him out of the woods. We didn't tell anyone because we believed in what the doctors said. We focused on getting Tim the best, most aggressive treatment so he would be back on his feet and all would be well. It should have taken no more than a few short months. That didn't happen as quickly as we anticipated. His care was so costly." Charisse went on to explain how the trucking business and Tim's treatment was the catalyst for a perfect storm of financial turmoil. In a short period of time, they accrued astronomical debt.

"Why didn't you tell us?" Jordan was baffled. He and Dorian were self-made men, determined to be wealthy to avoid living like they did after their father's passing. Either of them had more than enough to bail them out. Despite their strained relationship with Timothy, his construction management firm had helped pull their family out of grief and debt.

"We were managing it all until recently. Tim's major clients got wind of his condition and started excluding him from bids. With the possibility of him not being around, clients didn't want to chance their new contracts not knowing who would take over. Revenues plummeted. He didn't want me to ask you, but I told him we had no choice. He's a proud man—like you boys. Tim didn't want to burden you or mention the fact that I had anything to do with it. I invited Jordan to brunch so I could tell him the whole story. It's a bonus that you were able to join us, Dorian. I was going to you next."

"Wow!" Dorian said. "How's Tim doing?"

Charisse took a deep breath. Her posture slumped. "He's getting better."

Jordan didn't say anything but was relieved. Tim may not have been his favorite person, but he was good to his mother.

"How much do you need?" Dorian asked.

Charisse held her hands up. "I don't want a bailout. I want to make you an offer, part ownership for your investment."

"Does Tim know this?" Jordan sat back. "Does he want to be in business with his stepsons?" He couldn't read the expression on Dorian's face and wondered what he was thinking. He wasn't fond of the man but never wanted to see him suffer. He couldn't imagine his mother dealing with all of this on her own.

"Not yet. It took so much for him to agree to ask for a loan when we spoke to you the other night. I thought this would be a better idea. As of right now, the business is solely in Tim's name. I want to make sure that once you helped us out, you were able to get some kind of return on your investment if something happened to Tim. I'm trying to protect your interest and ours. I wanted to see what you had to say before telling him my plan."

Charisse looked between her boys. Jordan imagined his expression looked as pensive as Dorian's.

"How do you know that he'll agree to this?" Dorian asked.

"Because we really have no other options, and now that he's healthy again, I couldn't stand it if he lost the business he spent so many years building. This partnership would be much more beneficial than just a loan."

Jordan sat back and instinctively messaged his temples. He had no choice. He'd have to help his stepfather's business. Helping him was helping his mother. Despite his feelings for the man, he'd always been good to his mother. They were poor when he'd come around. As a business owner, his earnings afforded Charisse a much better life. And until now, their mother hadn't wanted for anything since Tim came into her life. However, the lives Jordan and Dorian created for themselves far exceeded what Tim had made possible. Their investment into his business wouldn't create a dent in their financial portfolios.

"Let's figure out the terms and get the attorneys to draw up the paperwork," Jordan said and turned to Dorian for his approval. His brother nodded.

Charisse exhaled so hard her chest heaved. She clasped her hands together with a clap. "Looks like we're going to be in business together. Now I just have to get Tim to agree to the new partnership. I'll need a little time."

Jordan's mother was a smart woman. He appreciated her desire to protect all of their interests. Jordan wondered if Tim's pride would get in the way.

Seven

Ivy wiped her clammy hands down the sides of her slacks again. She took three deep breaths and let them out slowly. Then she checked her reflection one more time. The smart, blue tailored suit fit perfectly. And she was happy with how her hair turned out—a full head of crinkly coils framed her head. She tugged on one in the front and it bounced right back into place. She felt excited, nervous and stressed. Each emotion fought to take the lead.

After grabbing her tote from the velvet bench in her bedroom, she headed down to the first floor. She paced, checked her smart watch and paced some more as she awaited her car service. She was too anxious to take the railroad or drive herself into the city.

Zoe had tried to get the meeting with Dale Billington

moved to later in the day while Jamie tried to get the producers to give them an earlier time. Dale wouldn't budge and was still adamant about making sure she met with Ivy specifically. The producers said their schedule was already very tight. At the last minute, they told her they could only meet a half hour earlier. This meant their meetings would still overlap. The distance between the offices was fifteen minutes so, no matter what, she would get back to her office after the meeting with Dale started.

She looked at her watch again and tried not to worry. Zoe promised to take good care of Dale but had urged Ivy to get to the office as soon as she possibly could.

Ivy's smart watch vibrated. The driver texted her letting her know he was outside. She grabbed her phone and designer tote bag and headed to the car. Inside the luxury vehicle, she laid her head against the seat headrest and closed her eyes, thankful that she wasn't at the wheel about to navigate New York.

The moment she arrived, Ivy spotted Jamie at the curbside. She opened the window and waved her hand as they pulled up. Jamie leaped and headed toward the car.

"You ready for this?" Jamie asked once the driver helped Ivy out.

"As ready as I'm ever going to be. I still can't believe it's happening." Ivy turned to the driver. "Thank you." He nodded and tipped his hat.

"Oh. It's happening, my dear," Jamie said.

Ivy struggled to keep up with Jamie's long-legged stride. She barely remembered entering the building and riding the elevator. Before she knew it, they were following a slim blonde woman inside a modern, all-white conference room. Even with white walls, table and chairs, the room managed to not look sterile. Her chest swelled with anticipation and her cheeks hurt because she couldn't keep herself from smiling. Yet she got nervous every time she glanced at her watch. She couldn't wait for the meeting to happen and wondered how soon it could be over.

"Mr. Chambers and Mr. Parks will be right in. Would you like water, coffee or tea?" the woman asked.

"Water will be fine," Ivy said.

"I'll take water too. Thank you," Jamie added.

The woman bought over two bottled waters and clear plastic cups.

Ivy didn't bother with the cups. She took the water bottle straight to her mouth, drank half and twisted the cap back on. Then she untwisted it again, not knowing what to do what her hands.

Ivy and Jamie turned their heads toward the door when they heard voices. A tall, fair-skinned gentleman walked in first, holding out his hand. They stood.

"Hello! I'm Anderson Parks." He shook Jamie's hand first, nodding as she said her name. Then he turned to Ivy and held out both hands. "And you're the Money Maven!" He took her hand between both of his and shook vigorously. "It's a pleasure to meet you."

"Pleasure to meet you too," she replied.

"Jordan Chambers."

Ivy heard the second man introduce himself to Jamie. She turned to see who the sultry voice belonged to, assuming he was as handsome as his baritone sound suggested. Smiling, she looked up and halted. She couldn't believe her eyes. It was the same man that had spilled wine and coffee on her just last week while she was in LA. She knew it was him. She'd never forget that gorgeous face belonging to such a clumsy man. She wondered if this was some kind of joke.

"Ivy," she heard Jamie whisper.

Jordan stood before her with his hand outstretched, waiting for her to shake it.

"Oh…um…sorry." She finally shook his hand. "Ivy Blackwell." Despite her memory of the ruined outfit, something sparked when his hand touched hers. She removed her hand from his quickly.

"Also known as the Money Maven," Jordan added. "Please, sit." He gestured toward the seat and sat in a chair across from Ivy.

Ivy thought she might have been mistaken about Jordan and brushed off what she thought she remembered. What were the chances it would be the same man? Who was she kidding? She remembered him being gorgeous. Tall, dark and handsome was an understatement. She took him in, attempting to be discreet as her gaze roved over his piercing hazel eyes, smooth brown skin, lightly shaved beard…and dimples. The man had *dimples*! Deep ones that she could get lost in. From the way his casual button-down shirt fit, she knew he was well acquainted with a gym somewhere. She felt Jamie tap her under the table.

"I believe Ms. Blackwell is just trying to figure out where she knows me from."

Jamie looked confused.

"Unfortunately, I caused a bit of a spill. Twice. One

of those times, I'm sure I ruined Ms. Blackwell's attire. Again, my apologies. I hope you'll forgive me."

That voice. She almost moaned it sounded so sexy. Ivy cocked her head sideways. Yep. It *was* him! "Is this some kind of joke, because I don't find it funny at all."

"What's going on here?" Jamie asked, looking around the room in confusion. It was apparent she was the only one who wasn't aware of what had happened.

"I assure you it isn't, Ms. Blackwell. I wanted to get that part out of the way so we could get on to business. Believe me, it's all pure coincidence."

Ivy looked from Jordan to Anderson. Anderson nodded—his attempt at confirming what Jordan had just said.

Anderson stood. "Ms. Blackwell. If I may?"

Ivy turned toward Anderson. She still wasn't sure how to feel. She had to get herself together. Jordan's good looks were distracting. She remembered the spark and knew she felt drawn to him despite the accident. Yet part of her wanted to be angry at Jordan. She felt as if she were being toyed with, but focused on keeping her composure in case this whole television opportunity was real.

Anderson cleared his throat before speaking again. He picked up the remote on the conference table and pointed it toward the flat screen on the wall. The television sprung to live. After another series of clicks, their logo was on the screen. Anderson started his presentation with a history of their company and a list of popular shows they'd produced. She knew many of them, some making her list of favorite shows to binge-watch whenever she found time.

"You've managed quite an impressive résumé." Images from her social media, speaking engagements and a few articles that she was featured in flashed across the screen as Anderson spoke. "Your social media presence is great. Your followers love you. We see you're representing major brands and have built a reputation as an authority in finance among women." He cleared his throat. "And, of course, we've been made aware that you have a new book coming out in a few weeks. We'd like to work with you to produce a television show featuring you helping people with poor financial management skills navigate large financial windfalls.

"And due to your expertise, we're happy to offer you producer credits as you help us streamline the content for the pilot. We have a few ideas for the title of the show and welcome your input there as well. As for now, here's our idea of how this will work…"

This *was* real. Ivy was so astonished she was having a hard time sitting still. Jordan and Anderson tag-teamed their presentation of show ideas for the first season and what they planned to present to the networks they were meeting with during the week. The more they shared, the more excited she became. By the time they asked her if she had any questions, she'd almost completely shaken off the angst she felt when she realized who Jordan was. However, she still felt drawn to Jordan. Ivy needed to get it together. She was never one to mix business with pleasure.

"We know this is short notice, but we'd like to propose something a bit unprecedented," Jordan said. "Due to the timing of the release of your book and our upcoming meetings with the networks this week, we'd like to expedite your contract with a contingency plan, giving us the okay to shop your ideas with the network while the agreement is being reviewed. If one of our networks is interested, we would then immediately get this show ready for the upcoming season so we can capitalize on the release of your book within the first few months. We're of course happy to consider any inconveniences in your compensation."

"We'll have to revisit what's in her publishing contract as it pertains to television rights," Jamie added.

"Wow. This is…a lot," Ivy murmured. "There's so much to consider. I need to speak to my team. When are your meetings with the networks?"

"Thursday and Friday," Jordan replied. "We can give you until noon on Thursday to respond and get this first part of the agreement to us so we can shop it at our meeting that afternoon." He paused. "And we've already outlined a treatment and series bible."

"What's that?" Ivy asked.

"Basically, a synopsis of the show with an outline of what each episode will be about," Anderson explained.

"Oh. Okay. Wow!"

"Any other questions?" Jordan paused while Jamie and Ivy looked at each other, then back at him.

Ivy's mind flooded with questions. "I need to absorb all of this. I'm sure I'll have plenty of questions after that."

"Great!" Jordan said. "Feel free to reach out to Anderson or me." Both men passed their business cards across the table.

"Thanks!" Ivy glanced at her watch as she reached for the business cards. More than an hour had passed.

Dale! Ivy stood abruptly. All eyes shifted to her. She planned to be out of this meeting within the hour. "I'm sorry. I have to get to another meeting. I look forward to reviewing the agreement that you send." She turned to Jamie. "Do you mind closing this out alone? I really have to go."

"Sure. You go ahead."

"Thanks!" she said, giving Jamie a quick hug. She shook Anderson's hand and then Jordan's. She left feeling his touch linger on her hand.

Ivy still wasn't sure what to think of all of this. Jordan…the show…the quick turnaround. But right now, she couldn't focus any more of her time or attention on that. She needed to get to Blackwell to catch whatever was left of the meeting with Dale.

Ivy called the driver to let him know she was on her way down. Maneuvering quickly, she exited the elevator and practically ran outside. As usual, New York City traffic was unforgiving. After ten minutes, she'd only traveled three blocks. Sirens blared and Ivy was sure she wasn't going to get to Blackwell in time.

Unable to sit still, she fidgeted until they arrived at the Blackwell offices twenty minutes later. The meeting was slated for an hour and had started an hour and twenty minutes ago. The second her driver stopped outside of the Blackwell building, she bolted out of the car, ran into the building and jabbed at the elevator call button until it came.

By the time she got upstairs the office was unusually quiet. She peeked into the conference room. It was empty. She headed for Zoe's office but she wasn't there. Ivy went to her office to drop her things. She plopped down into her office chair and twisted her head from side to side. Stress caused kinks to settle into her neck.

"Come in," Ivy responded to the soft knocks on her door.

Her father's secretary stuck her head in. "Mr. Blackwell would like to see you."

"I'll be right in," she said. When she heard the door close, she groaned. With the eerie silence of the office and the formal way in which her father's secretary had spoken, Ivy knew that this meeting wasn't going to be good. She felt a weight in the pit of her stomach as if a brick had settled there. Ivy stood. Placing one foot in front of the other, she made her way to her father's office.

Ivy tapped on his door but didn't wait for him to respond before cautiously stepping inside. She walked into another eerily silent atmosphere. Bill's narrowed eyes settled on her and stayed until she'd come all the way in. Zoe was already in the office and didn't look happy either. They exchanged knowing glances.

"Please. Sit!" Bill's tone was sharp. Ivy sat down slowly. "Now do you want to explain to me why we just lost one of the biggest possible accounts of the year?"

Ivy wished she could disappear.

Eight

Jordan's mind and body hadn't reconciled with the time difference. His body was still operating on West Coast time. This East Coast schedule was getting the best of him. With all the appointments that he and Anderson had on their calendars, including dinner meetings each night, Jordan felt exhausted.

Jordan dragged himself through the door of his Manhattan condominium, dropped his light jacket on the couch and headed to his en suite. For a moment, he stood at the entrance to his room and just stared at his custom bed. It was larger than the average king and looked inviting with the crisp, white down comforter and sheets. Jordan wanted to jump right in and wrap himself in the cocoon of comfort but that would have to wait.

Despite his fatigue, Jordan had to keep going. His

mind, on the other hand, wouldn't stop. He went over the meeting with Ivy in his head a thousand times. He remembered how beautiful she looked today and the first day he'd laid eyes on her. He'd felt something when they shook hands. Had Ivy felt it too? He'd handle business first but at some point he would find a way to get to know Ivy on a more personal level.

Tonight, he was scheduled to attend an event that he was invited to by one of the network executives. Christopher Yates, a friend and colleague from film school, was being honored as one of the youngest, most successful network executives in the industry. When he found out Jordan would still be in town, he had urged him to join him that evening as his guest—an invitation Jordan couldn't dare decline. The Forty Under Forty Awards event honored successful trailblazing professionals. Chris wasn't even thirty and had made a huge splash in the television and film industry.

Jordan trudged into the bathroom and turned on the water in the shower. Despite his age, he put on music from the nineties. His mother called him an old soul. Jordan adjusted the volume and R&B soul flowed from the speakers embedded throughout the master suite. The music energized him just enough. He bobbed his head as he dressed, wondering how long this second wind of his would last.

Dabbing on a bit of cologne, Jordan was ready to go. The car he ordered was waiting for him by the time he reached the lobby of his luxury building on Central Park West. Jordan loved the hustle and bustle of midtown, but appreciated the less busy, more residential atmosphere of the Upper West Side.

The event was taking place at one of the iconic hotels in Times Square. Jordan's driver pulled up and deposited him into the hands of one of the attendants, who greeted Jordan with a warm smile. Jordan pulled on the lapels of his black tux. There was a chill in the air. Perhaps he was no longer used to the autumn air in New York City. He made it a point to spend the cooler months in Los Angeles.

The elevator doors opened on the sixth floor of the hotel. Jordan stepped right into a bustling cocktail reception. High tables, three bars and tables full of delightful hors d'oeuvres were positioned around the space. Jordan headed to the bar, ordered himself a neat snifter of scotch and started looking for Chris. Texting him while he waited for his drink, Jordan let Chris know that he'd arrived.

Chris responded, letting him know to hang tight. He was in a room with the other honorees taking pictures and would be out as soon as he could. His friend gave him their table number to let him know where they would be seated. Soon after, Chris found him.

"Jordan!" Chris walked over to him, decked out in a well-fitting tux. "I'm glad you were able to make it." They shook hands.

"Wow. You're looking like quite the dapper guest of honor," Jordan teased, pointing at the rose tucked in Chris's breast pocket.

"Listen. I don't know what made them pick me for this honor," Chris grumbled, "but I'm going to make the best of it before anyone notices they made a mistake."

"Aw, you're too humble."

Out of the corner of his eye, Jordan thought he saw Ivy Blackwell.

Jordan continued talking to Chris but scanned the room to make sure his eyes weren't playing tricks on him. He looked down at the drink in his hand and made a note to himself to keep his distance and then laughed to himself. There would be *no* way to recover from spilling his drink on her a third time.

Jordan heard the unmistakable sound of Ivy's voice. The warm, soothing tone was familiar to him. It flowed through him. Whatever that feeling was, it felt good. Jordan furrowed his eyebrows at his body's response. What was that? Why had her voice sounded that way? Jordan shook his head as if it would rid him of the effects of this beautiful, unnerving woman.

Turning toward the voice, Jordan spotted her before she spotted him. His eyes narrowed a bit as he took her in. Like the first time he saw her at the premiere, she looked stunning. Her black sequin dress dropped off her shoulder, hugged every curve of her beautiful body and flared around her feet, cascading in a waterfall of delicate shimmering fabric. Her hair, loaded with full beautiful natural coils, was pulled up on one side. She was flawless. Jordan felt some kind of butterfly action in his stomach. He couldn't remember ever feeling that before.

Ivy's beauty was undeniable, but if all went well, they would be entering into a business agreement. There was no room for whatever this was he was feeling. Besides, the only thing he knew about this woman was what he'd read online. Jordan recalled her expression when she realized he was the same guy that spilled drinks on her twice. The excited smile that she entered the meeting with fell faster than a shooting star.

Jordan took her in for several long moments and noticed she was wearing a corsage. Ivy was an honoree like Chris. Jordan found himself walking toward her and wondered what he would say. The internal question caught him off guard. Despite the fact that he hadn't dated in a while, Jordan had never been at a loss for words when it came to women. He wasn't the player he used to be but he certainly wasn't shy around the opposite sex.

The closer Jordan got, the more he noticed her smooth brown skin. He wondered how soft her shoulders must have felt. The curve of her neck enticed him. He continued to survey Ivy. Full ruby red lips spread into a cordial smile lifting up lovely high cheekbones toward her doe eyes. This woman was absolutely gorgeous. Her looks would certainly help boost the show. Hollywood and viewers loved beautiful women.

Jordan had been studying her so closely he saw the sudden shift in her posture go from graceful to rigid. Ivy's sculptured back stiffened. Her chin lifted. And from her profile, he could see her smile melt and the set of her jaw tighten. Someone must have said something to upset her. For the first time since he started in her direction, he took notice of the people around him. He noticed two women and one man. Who was that man? Could he have been her significant other? Jordan rolled his eyes toward the ceiling. He shouldn't care who the man was.

He had second thoughts about continuing his approach now that she seemed bothered but he kept heading in her direction. Just when he'd made it to her, Ivy lifted the bottom of her dress and turned abruptly. He halted, leaving a short distance between them. Their eyes met briefly, fire in hers, questioning in his. She blinked twice and recognition seemed to set in. She inhaled a slight gasp.

"Oh. Hello, Jordan." Ivy's tone was clipped. She looked at his hand at the drink he was holding and then back at his face.

Jordan raised a brow. "Miss Blackwell," he greeted smoothly. He drew his drink back as if to let her know she didn't have to worry about it landing on her beautiful gown.

"I'm sorry but now is not a good time." She turned to a young man holding a camera next to her. "Come on, Radcliffe." She stepped around Jordan. "Enjoy the event, Mr. Chambers." Then Ivy walked away, leaving Jordan to wonder what has just happened.

One thing was for sure…her icy greeting had definitely given him pause. It was obvious that something had just happened that had the potential to ruin an evening that was supposed to be all about her. Then Jordan remembered that since he'd met Ivy, every encounter they'd shared had been far from cheerful. Granted, she had reason to be annoyed with him the first two times. He wondered if the woman ever flashed a genuine smile. Was she generally grumpy? Still, none of that kept his body from involuntarily responding to her presence. He needed to get a grip on all those unexpected reactions. It was clear that Ivy wasn't interested in him in any way. Now he wondered if she was even a nice person.

Nine

This week wasn't going well *at all*. Ivy was exhausted. Her dad was upset with her because he blamed her for losing a huge client. And now on a night that was supposed to be a great celebration, Ivy was trying to keep her composure. This Forty Under Forty Awards event sure wasn't turning out to be as festive as she'd looked forward to.

Ivy couldn't believe what had just happened. Her feet couldn't carry her away fast enough. Her branding assistant, Jess, and sister-in-law, Zoe, were fast on her heels. Ivy's anger made her eyes sting but she wouldn't dare allow one tear to drop in front of all those people at the reception. Thankful that she'd reserved a room in that hotel for the night, she jabbed the elevator button and immediately felt like the elevator took too long to arrive. Jess remained silent but Zoe rubbed her back.

The reception was just getting started and she and the other honorees should have been mingling with guests, but Ivy had to get away. She'd ordered Radcliff to stop taking pictures and filming. Her anger flared way too hot to be on camera. A fellow influencer and honoree had just insulted her, literally calling her a pretentious bitch in the middle of the reception. It caused a slight commotion when Ivy tried her best to respond without stooping to that woman's level. Ivy didn't understand why but this woman, Kenya Brown, seemed to have it out for her. Although this was the first time she'd seen her in person, it wasn't the first snide remark she'd slid in Ivy's direction. Ivy's social media team had to delete comments from her in the past. However, she had never resorted to name-calling.

Ivy had swallowed, bringing herself back to the present before directing a glare toward Kenya and saying, "It's obvious that my existence offends you. It's certainly not my fault that you don't believe you measure up. How unfortunate." It was then that she turned abruptly and looked right into the eyes of Jordan Chambers. His presence surprised her. Ivy hadn't known how long he'd been there or how much he'd overheard. She'd hoped he hadn't heard much. Ivy was never condescending but this woman had gone too far and in public. Ivy had done nothing to her personally.

Turning and looking into Jordan's handsome face had sliced through her anger for a quick moment. Instantly she had been fully aware of how gorgeous he was. His timing was always horrible, yet something inside of her was happy to see him.

After greeting him, she'd looked around and saw that

several people had cell phones turned in her direction. She needed to get away. She was a Blackwell. She was also a public figure and wasn't about to give people a show for them to post and get likes at her expense. Her parents would have never let her live that down.

"I need a minute," she had said to Zoe, who was standing by her side when all of this had gone down.

Zoe and Jess headed up with her to her room. Ivy was glad she'd booked a suite when she found out about the event. She knew going upstairs at the end of the night would be much more convenient than traveling back to Long Island after all of the festivities. Plus, she had a meeting with Dale in the morning and wanted to be fresh for that. A short commute would definitely help.

"What was that woman's problem?" Zoe asked in the elevator.

"I really don't know. I recognized her from her Instagram page. She's another influencer but I have no idea why she's so fixated on me."

"These things happen on social media sometimes," Jess mused. "It's a way for a lesser-known influencer to gain popularity."

"We need to block her completely," Ivy said as she held her key card up to her hotel room door.

"Please do," Zoe said. "Take a moment to gather yourself and let's head back down." She flopped down on the couch.

Jess disappeared momentarily and came back with bottles of water for Zoe and Ivy.

"And who was that guy that came up to you?" Zoe asked, taking a sip from her bottle.

"Oh!" Ivy sighed and dropped her shoulders. "That

was Jordan Chambers, the producer that wants to do the show with me."

"Oh!" Zoe said. "He's a good-looking man. Did you know he would be here?"

"I didn't. Seeing him was a complete surprise."

"I'm glad you managed to keep your cool. We don't want you getting the wrong kind of press." Zoe parked her hands on her hips. "I should have socked her right in the mouth for you. Then it wouldn't have reflected negatively on you!" Zoe and Jess laughed.

Ivy smiled at Zoe's comment but her focus was now on Jordan Chambers. Saying his name bought his handsome face back to the forefront of her mind. He was the last person she expected to see, as usual. He just kept showing up in the most interesting ways. Ivy wondered if he'd caught her gasp when she saw him. She hadn't expected her breath to catch at the sight of his gorgeous face. Now that she thought about it, she hadn't been very friendly toward him. Hopefully she'd have a chance to make up for her cold greeting and swift departure. Plus, she didn't want to jeopardize her chances at working with him on the show.

She'd been thinking about the show proposal. Actually, if she was being honest, she'd been thinking about much more than that. And right now, thoughts of Jordan made her less angry. She remembered his smooth dark skin, piercing brown eyes, full luscious lips and tall, athletic stance. Their first two encounters were less than desirable, but she couldn't deny even then that the man was a majestic work of art.

"Ivy!"

"Huh?" She turned toward Zoe, who exchanged a raised-brow glance with Jess.

"I just asked if you were okay to go back down now. It's almost time to line up with the rest of the awardees."

Ivy hadn't heard a word. "Oh…yeah." Thinking about Jordan had stolen all of her senses. She stood, finished the remnants of her water and huffed. "Okay. Let's go."

"It's your night, sissy! We won't let anything or anyone ruin this for you," Zoe said. "Ready?" She stepped to Ivy and held out her elbow toward her.

"You're right." Ivy linked her arm in Zoe's.

"And I meant what I said earlier. If she says one more nasty word, I'll punch her right in that overly bronzed nose of hers."

All three women laughed.

When they stepped off the elevator on the same floor as the ballroom, one of the event managers rushed to Ivy.

"Ms. Blackwell!" a slender woman said urgently. "We've addressed Ms. Brown and advised that her behavior was both unacceptable and unbecoming of an honoree. You shouldn't have any more issues tonight. We sincerely apologize for her behavior and please let us know if you have any further issues with her tonight."

"Thank you," Ivy murmured politely. She was glad she held her composure.

Ivy smiled, held her head up and waltzed toward the waiting area where the rest of the honorees were now standing. Despite how the publicist took care of the situation, something told Ivy she'd still have to keep an eye on Kenya Brown.

From the corner of her eye, Ivy spotted Jordan.

"Give me one second," she said to Jess and Zoe.

Ivy walked over to Jordan, who was talking to one of the other honorees. She believed his name was Chris. "Jordan?" Ivy got his attention.

"Ivy." Jordan smiled. Ivy's stomach fluttered. Most would consider that bright-toothed smile to be professional, but for some reason, it looked incredibly sexy to her.

"Sorry to interrupt. Can I speak to you for a quick moment?" She nodded politely, acknowledging Chris.

"Sure. Excuse me, Chris." Jordan followed Ivy a few feet, placing distance between them, the network executive and the rest of the honorees.

"I just wanted to apologize. My greeting earlier was less than cordial. I had a situation…arise that I had to address immediately."

Jordan held up both hands. "No need to apologize. I understand."

"Thanks. Maybe I'll buy you dinner or something to make up for it if things get started with the show you've proposed."

"You mean *when*, not if," Jordan said.

"Yes. When we get started with the show."

Silence expanded between them for a moment. Just when it started to get uncomfortable, Jordan asked, "Why wait? How about a celebratory drink after the event tonight? That would suffice."

"Oh. Um…" Ivy paused. His question was unexpected. She would love to have a drink with him, but wondered if she should.

"It's okay if you're not available. I was just…thinking…"

Ivy *was* available. She was staying at the hotel. Alone. Zoe and the rest of the family were heading back to their respective homes after the event. "I guess that would be fine. I'm actually staying here tonight so I wouldn't have to travel back home after this was over. I knew I'd be tired. So…sure."

"Great!" Jordan said. "We can meet at the bar, or one of the local places nearby. See you later." He tipped an imaginary hat and flashed that gorgeous smile of his.

"Yes. See you then." Her stomach fluttered at his smile. "I'm really a nice person." For some reason, Ivy felt a need to add that statement.

A bemused look spread across Jordan's face but he didn't respond. After a simple nod he started off before turning back to say, "And congratulations."

"Thank you," Ivy said, smiling back at him. She didn't move right away. Instead, she just stood there, watching Jordan leave. His gait was masculine and confident, just the way she liked. Rolling her eyes at her inner thoughts, Ivy snickered and made her way to the line moments before being called to make her entrance. Sporting a narrowed glare, Kenya watched her the whole time. Ivy ignored her. She'd deal with that pest later. This was *her* night and Zoe was right. She couldn't let Kenya ruin it. As excited as she was about this honor, she felt even more excitement growing inside her belly in anticipation of having a drink with Jordan later that evening.

Ten

Jordan didn't expect to enjoy himself as much in Ivy's company. He'd pegged her as cordial but also rigid.

As they sat in a set of posh lounge chairs near the bar in the hotel lobby, Ivy told him about the encounter with the woman, Kenya, just before he had approached her. She also apologized for not being so nice when she greeted him. That really seemed to bother her, especially the fact that the woman called her pretentious. Ivy insisted that she was anything *but* pretentious. Jordan made note to keep his preconceived notion about her to himself forever.

Several times, as she recounted the story, Jordan found himself getting lost in studying her smooth brown skin, beautiful full lips and perfectly sculptured cheekbones. The rise of her neck was regal, almost majestic. He felt like he was in the presence of a queen. And that raspy voice of hers made her conversation sound like a song. Her hair, full and unruly, blossomed from her head in a perfect spray of curls that framed her face.

"Enough about me. Tell me more about yourself, Mr. Chambers. How did you get into television?"

Jordan picked up his snifter of scotch. "I've always been fascinated by movies and shows. I thought about being an actor but quickly realized that being in front of the camera wasn't for me."

"As handsome as you are, I'm sure you would have done well," Ivy said but then her smile dropped immediately as if she hadn't meant to say that. "I'm sorry. I wasn't trying to…"

Her embarrassment tickled him. He watched her shift in her seat and take sip of her own scotch. That intrigued him too. A woman that wasn't afraid of whiskey.

"Thank you," he said. "I just enjoyed being behind the camera much more. I like making up stories and decided to go to film school." Jordan sipped. "NYU."

"That's fantastic!"

"I wanted to go to UCLA, but I didn't want to be that far from my mom. Plus, NYU was doling out some really good scholarships at the time."

"So, you live in LA now?"

"Both. I have a place there and one here. My mom is still here."

"Got it."

"And you? What's your story?" Jordan asked. "At least the part you're willing to tell." He'd meant to be flirty…was testing the waters.

Ivy's smile gave him the response he had been looking for. She shared some of her background and talked about the new initiatives at Blackwell, which ended up being the catalyst for speaking and becoming an influencer. This woman was all kinds of intriguing, Jordan thought to himself. She was smart, innovative, ambitious and insanely sexy. Why didn't she have someone special in her life?

"Wow!" Jordan whispered when she finished speaking. "I have to ask. Are you single?"

Ivy sniffed out a laugh and playfully rolled her eyes toward the ceiling. "Yep."

"Why?" He really wanted to understand why someone hadn't tried to make her their wife yet.

Ivy side-eyed him. With her glass to her lips she asked, "You've been talking with my mother?"

That made him laugh. "You know what?" He held both arms up in surrender. "I'm sorry. Now I sound like my own mother, and yours too, I'm sure. Forgive me. I didn't mean to pry."

"Just busy." She answered him anyway. "That's all. No time for dating. I take it you're riding the single train too?"

"Yep." He raised his glass and took a sip.

"Why?" Ivy mocked and chuckled.

"Touché. Busy. Like you." Jordan looked directly into her eyes. For a moment, they were suspended in each other's gaze.

After a few seconds, both looked away and focused on the drinks in their hand. Silenced settled between them. Ivy looked around the bar like she was avoiding his gaze.

Maybe her being single made her even more attractive. Jordan cleared his throat, took one last sip and put his empty tumbler down on the table between them. Then he sat back in his chair and cuffed his chin in his hand. He felt warmth spread inside of him. It could have been the whiskey. More likely, it was probably his body's response to Ivy. The longer he sat with her, the more drawn he was to her.

Jordan summed Ivy up. Beyond the curves, beauty, melodic voice and strong presence, he liked her cool demeanor and could tell she had a take-charge kind of attitude. She wasn't exactly a girlie-girl, but a feminine power emanated from her. He didn't expect that from her after doing his research. But then again, he had just seen the glamorous highlight reel posted on social media. He realized he didn't know much about the real Ivy Blackwell at all.

Seeing her wrap her pretty red lips around that glass of whiskey created a feeling in his core that Jordan had never experienced but truly enjoyed. Most of the women in his life happened to enjoy wine or mixed drinks. None were ever bourbon or whiskey connoisseurs. If it hadn't been for the fact that they may be working together soon, he'd ask her out. Like Ivy, he had no time for dating, but wanted to get to know more about this fascinating woman.

Ivy leaned toward him to speak over the crowd that was growing louder. "It's getting pretty packed in here," she said, placing her empty glass down on the table as well.

Jordan took that as his cue. The night was ending even though he didn't want it to. "Yeah." He noticed there were lots more people in the lounge now than there was when they first arrived.

He'd been so into Ivy he hadn't realized the place had filled up. It seemed that someone turned up the volume. He noticed the background noise now, though. Blended languages and conversations created a buzzing backdrop.

Jordan waited to see what Ivy would do next. He wasn't going to be the first to stand. That would mark their time together as done and he refused to be the one to end their evening.

"Maybe there's someplace quieter?" he suggested huskily, leaning to her so she could hear him.

"I'd invite you to my room, Mr. Chambers, if I could trust you to behave…"

At first Jordan wasn't sure if she was joking or not. He questioned her statement with his furrowed brows and a squint.

"Easy, cowboy. I'm teasing. You're welcome to join me for another drink if you're not ready to head home. I have a great single malt up there that my sister-in-law bought me tonight. I'd like to try it out and I usually don't drink alone." Ivy looked around. "At least we will be able to hear each other talk."

Jordan smiled. She was witty and direct. He liked that about her. "I'd be happy to join you," he said, thrilled that she wasn't ready to end the night either.

Inside of Ivy's penthouse, he got comfortable in the living room, while she retreated to the bedroom to change out of her fancy dress. She returned in leggings and an Ivy League hoodie and looked just as alluring as before.

Jordan had never considered a woman in a hoodie sexy until now.

"Neat or on the rocks?" she asked, approaching the minibar. She picked up the bottle and looked over the label.

"Neat works for me."

"I noticed that about you," Ivy said, taking two glasses to the sink at the wet bar to rinse them out. "And I agree. Especially with a single malt. I don't want to water down the flavor." She poured about an inch of the amber liquid into each glass and handed one to Jordan. "Wanna sit on the balcony? It's cool but still really nice out."

Jordan stood from his seated position on the couch and held out his hand, gesturing for her to go first. He followed closely behind.

Outside, they sat watching the stars that lit up the velvet sky while letting the autumn breeze wash over them. Moments passed without either of them speaking. There was nothing uncomfortable about the silence. Jordan basked in it as well as the breeze and his extended time with Ivy.

Taking another sip, he held out his glass and looked at it. He swirled the liquid around. "This is good."

"Isn't it." Ivy's voice was relaxed.

To Jordan her voice seemed deeper. Sexier. "So why don't you have a significant other…?" Yep. He went there again.

Jordan watched a smile spread across her pretty face in the moonlight. Ivy chuckled.

"According to my last boyfriend, I'm not a good girlfriend."

Jordan hissed. "That was harsh."

"Humph. I agreed with him at the time."

"Seriously?" Jordan reared his head back. A sense of alarm shot through him.

"I really wasn't a good girlfriend—for *him*. Why do you ask?"

"I want to know. You're beautiful, smart, you like single malts." He shrugged and tilted his head matter-of-factly. Both of them laughed.

"Ha! Cute. I didn't meet his idea of what a girlfriend was supposed to be. I guess I'm…different. Oh. And I was way too busy for him. He complained that I never spent enough time with him. That was before I started doing all of this social media stuff and became an author. Now I may be doing a television show."

"*Will* be doing one. Not may be," Jordan corrected her.

"Yes. Okay. Will! Now that I'll also be doing a television show." She looked over at Jordan and smiled. "We never would have made it work. This would all be too much for him."

Jordan shook his head and sighed. "I never understood men who had issues with ambitious women."

"I'm okay with being single." Ivy sat back in her chair.

"Me too," he said. At least he was until now. Unraveling all that Ivy Blackwell represented made him want to know more. She was soft and strong. Elegant and grounded. The dichotomy of her fascinated him.

"What will your next boyfriend be like?" Jordan continued to push the issue. He wanted know.

"Whenever that happens," Ivy said with a wry laugh. Then, growing serious, she tilted her head to the side, seeming to think about Jordan's question. After a while she continued. "A friend," she said quietly, looking past him. "I want my next boyfriend to be my friend."

Jordan felt something heavy in her response. It made him want to hug her.

"What about you? What will your next one be like?" She spun the inquisition back to him.

Jordan thought for a moment. "Present," he said, following her lead on heavy responses. He thought about his ex. Even when they were together, she was never truly present with him. Maybe that's what was so intriguing about being with Ivy. In their short time together, she was fully there with him.

"Hmm. Nice." She sipped from her glass and looked out over the skyline.

The two sat silently for several moments. Then Ivy turned to him and stared directly into his eyes. Her voice was soft. "Maybe the next ones won't leave these voids."

The weight of her response settled between them. The acknowledgment of both of them being unfulfilled linked them in that moment. Ivy hadn't taken her eyes off him. Returning her gaze, he summed things up again. That's why they both worked hard. They had voids to fill.

Desire for Ivy rose in his chest, nearly choking him. He looked at her pretty lips and wanted to kiss away the sadness in her eyes. There was something else in her eyes. It resembled yearning. The same that was in his soul. He hadn't noticed it until that moment.

Compelled by all that he was feeling, Jordan put his glass down, stepped over to Ivy and closed the distance between them. He knelt down and touched her chin. She continued looking straight into his eyes. He studied her. Jordan wanted to press his lips against hers but not without permission. Something about this beautiful, captivating woman drew him in. He leaned closer but knew he couldn't be the one to initiate a kiss. Blinking, he tried to tamp down the craving swirling inside of him. Then Ivy lifted her chin. Her lips were mere inches from his. Jordan willed himself to be still. They were caught in each other's gaze. Ivy's lips parted slightly. She closed her eyes and came closer, inch by inch, until her lips touched his.

When their lips finally connected, a hot trail blazed through his belly. Taking her face in his hands, Jordan kissed Ivy with a hunger he didn't realize he'd possessed. Before he knew it, they were standing, and Jordan slid his arms around her waist. Ivy's hands rubbed up and down his torso as they devoured one another in the kiss. Breathless, they continued. Jordan felt himself grow hard inside his slacks and then pressed intimately against her. He had to stop. If not, he would drown in his own desire. It took all of his strength for him to pull away. When he did, they just stared at each other again. He wanted more and could tell she did too.

"Thank you," he whispered.

She returned a breathy, "No. Thank you."

"I better go."

Ivy pressed her lips together and nodded in agreement.

Slowly, Jordan removed his hands from around her waist. The moment he released her, he was reminded of the coolness of the night. He backed away to keep himself from reaching for her again. Ivy touched her lips, cleared her throat and then walked past him. He followed her to the door. She opened it, swallowed and gave him a small smile. Jordan ran his thumb across her cheek and touched her lip. He couldn't help it. Just one more touch of that supple skin was all he needed to take with him.

This time, Jordan was the one who swallowed and cleared his throat. His eyes were on hers. Finally, he nodded and willed himself out of her hotel room. The door connected behind him slowly. He stood still and took a long, deep breath and pondered all that could have happened.

Eleven

"You *what*?" Zoe screamed and immediately covered her mouth.

"Zoe! Shhh." Ivy looked around the restaurant at all the eyes staring back at them. It was just before nine in the morning.

"You kissed him?" This time Zoe whispered. "Who initiated the kiss?"

"Me. Well, both of us," Ivy admitted. "He came over to me and leaned in but stopped. I took that as him asking permission and by then I wanted to kiss him too, so I sealed the deal."

"Then what happened?" Zoe asked.

Ivy looked at her watch. Dale would be arriving any minute.

"Nothing. He left after that and boy am I glad he did.

I'm not sure what would have happened. There was so much chemistry between us!"

"So, are you going to see him again?" her sister-in-law asked.

"Here's the crazy part, Zoe. I don't even have a number for him. I'd have to call my agent to get in touch with him."

"You have got to be kidding me." Zoe covered her sharp bark of laughter with her hand. She shook her head. "Do you *want* to see him again?"

"I'd like to but I don't think it will make sense to bother. He has a place here in the city but spends most of his time in LA. His schedule is crazy busy and so is mine. Not to mention mine is about to get busier with this book coming out and I can't forget about the show. He's convinced that it's going to happen. If we hook up, that will probably make things more awkward."

"You're right. But it's been forever since you dated."

"That's probably why I kissed him. I forgot what it was like to kiss a man." Ivy threw her head back and laughed.

"I'm sure!" Zoe said sarcastically and laughed too. "If he called you, *would* you see him again?"

"I doubt it. I don't like mixing business with pleasure…"

"That's fair! Okay. Let's talk about Dale." Zoe clasped her hands together and changed the subject.

The two of them had a half hour to prepare for their meeting with Dale. Ivy wanted to smooth things over with her and try to recover the deal.

"You know I don't get nervous, but I'm anxious about this meeting."

"I know. Dale was pretty upset about what happened. She felt slighted. I did everything I could to convince her that it was okay that you weren't there. But she wasn't buying it. Dale wants to deal with you, not me. She's not like our other clients."

"I know. Dad still seems angry with me. I also think working with Dale will be good for so many reasons. First of all, her investment portfolio is huge. Also, I'd love to pull her in on some of my speaking engagements."

"Maybe that will win her over," Zoe said. "I believe that's why she was adamant about working with you. She loves the spotlight. Does she know about the book?"

"No," Ivy said. "Let's go over what we want to say. We'll tag team on these items." She pointed to the bulleted points in her notes.

Ivy and Zoe went over their game plan until Dale made her entrance. She walked in, dressed in sky blue from head to toe—a fedora, light jacket to ward off the autumn breeze, blouse, trousers and pumps. Dale stepped in and looked around as if waiting for one of the waiters to come take her jacket. Ivy waved her over. She lifted her chin acknowledging Ivy before prancing in their direction. Ivy and Zoe shared a quick glance and stifled a laugh. If anyone was pretentious, it was certainly Dale Billington.

"Ladies!" Dale nodded at both of them as they stood.

"Good morning, Dale," Zoe said.

"I'm so glad you could make it," Ivy added.

Dale looked behind her as if someone was going to pull out her chair. She huffed and slid it back and sat down. "I squeezed you in. I don't have much time. I have another meeting downtown after this."

"These busy schedules are a killer, right?" Zoe sympathized. "Will you have something to eat?"

"Yes, but something quick. I'm starving."

Zoe waved the waiter over. Ivy and Zoe ordered something simple from the menu. But Dale, on the other hand, required avocado toast and rearranged everything else that came with it to fit to her liking. "I only want the eggs if they're cage free. Please put my seasoning on the side. I'd like extra tomatoes, and orange juice only if it's freshly squeezed. And please bring me a steaming cup of coffee ASAP." She practically shooed the waiter away before turning her attention back to Ivy and Zoe.

"I'm going to cut to the chase, Dale. I'll start by apologizing for being late for the meeting. I'll have to let you in on a secret to explain why but you have to promise not to say a word to anyone."

The woman raised both brows and sat up straighter. "Hmm. Confidentiality. I can handle that."

Ivy explained everything. The more she talked, the wider Dale smiled. By the time she was done talking about the book and the television show, Dale was smiling from ear to ear.

Ivy ended by saying, "With that said, I think we will be able to work together in more ways than one. I see it being mutually beneficial."

Dale leaned aside while the waiter placed their breakfast in front of them. "I knew you were a gem. Congratulations and I forgive you." After chewing a bit of avocado, Dale asked a few more questions about Ivy's new endeavors. She seemed genuinely interested. "This all sounds so wonderful."

"I'm really excited." Ivy glanced over at Zoe, who looked like she'd released a breath she'd been holding in for hours.

She was getting ready to dig into her meal when she heard Dale say, "But I'll have to think about transferring my portfolio to Blackwell…"

Ivy and Zoe exchanged glances once again.

"Can I ask why?" Zoe asked.

"Sure. I completely support you in all of these wonderful opportunities. However, my concern is this— with all that Ivy will have on her plate, leaving you, Zoe, to do most of the managing of my portfolio, which is quite significant, I wonder how much attention you will be able to pay to my investments. It's your combined brilliance that attracted me to Blackwell and without you—" Dale looked at Zoe and then Ivy "—managing my assets as a team, then who will? You sold me on your financial savvy. With you out of the picture, I'm not so sure about this." Dale cut her knife into a slice of her avocado toast as if what she had just said didn't make Ivy's heart drop into her stomach.

For a quick moment, Ivy was at a loss for words. Her plan backfired. Instead of using her opportunities to secure the business, it seemed to be the one thing that could drive the woman's business away.

"Rest assured, Dale, that our savvy is still very much part of the strategy for our women's investment initiatives and will especially be integral to managing your portfolio."

"I'm sure you believe that."

Ivy kept her composure as she watched Dale enjoy her breakfast. She'd lost her own appetite.

"Dale, I will always be part of the Blackwell team. My book tour will only be a few weeks and my understanding about the show is that it will require only a couple of weeks of filming. I can assure you that your investments will be safe with us as it is for all of our amazing clients."

Dale shopped chewing and sat back.

No one spoke for several moments. Ivy hoped a "yes" was brewing.

"I'll have to give this some thought," Dale finally said.

"Of course! I know you're busy. But how about we give you a moment to think about it. In the meantime, we'll provide you with a few details about our recommendations for your portfolio and we can schedule to meet in about three weeks," Ivy suggested.

"I'll have my assistant connect yours to get something on our calendars," Zoe added.

Dale inhaled and exhaled with a groan. "I'll take a look at the information." She didn't commit to anything else. "By far these people have the best avocado toast in the city." Dale closed her eyes and savored the flavor.

"Yes. Their food is pretty good," Ivy said, forcing a smile but feeling deflated.

Dale looked at her cell phone. "Oh! I need to get going." She wiped her mouth, put her napkin down and pushed back from the table.

Zoe and Ivy stood with her. "It's always a pleasure spending time with you," Ivy said.

Dale held out her arms and Ivy stepped into her embrace. Then she hugged Zoe and gave them both air kisses.

"Thanks for breakfast, ladies. I'll be in touch." Dale dialed someone on her cell phone. "I'll be right there," she told them and pranced out of the restaurant the same way she'd pranced in.

Once again, Zoe and Ivy looked at each other. Zoe shook her head as they sat back down. Neither of them had touched their food. Ivy grunted.

"We're not giving up," Zoe declared.

"No. We're not," Ivy agreed but Dale's words stuck with her. Her concern was valid. How was Ivy supposed to manage it all? She had been so sure they were going to close this deal with Dale over breakfast, but now who knew? Ivy sighed. Dale Billington would have become their biggest female client. Her business would have led to other big clients. Her dad, Bill, was expecting them to come back with a sealed deal as well.

The scariest thought was, what if other clients started to feel the same way? She'd promised her father that taking on this extra stuff wouldn't affect her work at Blackwell. But it did—more and more each day.

Ivy heard Zoe ask the waitress to wrap their food. She then said that she was ordering a car to take them back to the office. Thoughts about losing clients continued to plague Ivy as they paid the bill and headed out of the restaurant.

While they were waiting for the car to arrive, Ivy's phone vibrated. She checked her text messages and then opened her Instagram app. Her largest number of followers were on Instagram. Checking it regularly had become a habit. In a heap of direct messages, she spotted one that had just come in from Jordan. Ivy remembered their kiss. She felt his lips on hers. He'd taken her breath away. Although she hadn't planned to see him again, she smiled.

Twelve

After kissing Ivy, Jordan headed back to his apartment in Manhattan. He'd slept better that night than he had in days. Is that what a woman did for a man who hadn't dated in a while? Yet early the next morning, as he prepared for his flight back to LA, he scolded himself for succumbing to his desires. He'd left at just the right time. Any longer and who knows what could have happened.

Jordan didn't want things to get awkward between the two of them. He really wanted this show to work. Networks were hungry for content and he needed to make sure he could continuously supply them with innovative show ideas. Since the explosion of all of the subscription television services, business had been wild. Things moved fast, and to stay on top of the game, his company had to keep up with the frenzied pace or get left behind.

As he packed, he wondered if he should tell Anderson about what had happened. He was never a man who would kiss and tell, but this could interfere with business, and if it did, Anderson would need to know. Jordan decided to keep his colleague on a need-to-know basis.

Thoughts of Ivy invaded his mind all the way to the airport. He wanted to call her. Jordan didn't expect to start a whole relationship based on one kiss, but he also didn't want to seem like a jerk either. He wasn't the type to kiss and disappear. If nothing ever happened between them again, he needed to at least make sure things between them were going to be okay moving forward.

Picking up his phone, Jordan realized he didn't have a telephone number for Ivy. Anderson had been in contact with her publisher and agent. Neither of them had called the Money Maven directly. Jordan tapped his Instagram icon and left a direct message.

Good morning, Ivy. Congratulations again on your award. It was great hanging with you last night. Please know that I don't have any weird expectations after yesterday. I look forward to working with you. Let's do lunch the next time you're in LA or the next time I'm in New York. Take care.

Jordan hoped his message would be received the way he intended. Simple and direct was what he was going for. He'd love to kiss her again and do so much more, but didn't want to assume too much or cause any issues while they worked together. All the same, Jordan was going to cherish that kiss in case he never got to feel Ivy's lips on his again.

Jordan pulled out his laptop in the airport lounge to get some work done while he waited for his plane to board. He checked his phone a few times to see if Ivy had responded. The last time, he laughed at himself. How had she gotten to him so quickly that he was checking his phone for her to reply? Sighing, he picked up his phone one last time. There was still no reply to his direct message. More than two hours had passed.

Jordan sent one last message. I realized we never exchanged numbers. I figured it would make sense since we will be working together soon. Take care.

Jordan was done—allegedly. No more messages and no more checking to see if she messaged him back. It was time to move on. All they shared was a kiss. It was an incredible kiss but it was just one. It didn't mean anything. She may never respond and that was okay with Jordan. He needed to get back to work. There were tons of emails awaiting his attention.

Despite his attempt to focus, his mind kept wandering to thoughts of Ivy. Flashes of her in her beautiful gown played in his mind's eye. Then he saw her curled up in the chair on her balcony dressed in a hoodie and leggings, nursing a glass of scotch. The last image enticed him as much as her in the gorgeous gown. Thoughts and visuals accompanied him all the way back to LA.

"Over here!" Jordan heard Anderson say when he exited the terminal at LAX.

He shielded his eyes from the beaming West Coast

sun. Spotting Anderson, he lifted his chin and headed toward him. "What's up, man?" They shook hands.

Jordan tapped the trunk. Anderson popped it open with his key fob. After dumping his bag inside, Jordan jumped into the passenger seat of Anderson's Aston Martin.

"How was the rest of your trip? The family is all good?" his friend asked as he pulled into the line of cars heading toward the airport exit.

"They're all good," Jordan said, looking out the window. He loved New York but really missed LA whenever he left.

"The stepfather too?" Anderson asked.

Jordan raised a brow. He referred to that man as his mother's husband, not his stepdad. "He's fine, I guess."

"You decided not to help?"

"I actually never spoke to him about it. Dorian and I met with my mother. She wanted a little time to speak to Timothy."

"So, you've decided to help him out."

"I'm going to help my *mother* out."

"Got it."

For a while Jordan sat quietly, taking in the California landscape. "So. Guess who I saw last night?"

"Who?"

"Ivy Blackwell. She was at the same awards ceremony as Chris. She was getting an award too."

"Cool! See I told you. She's hot right now. All of this will help with the show. I hope the network moves fast on this. We need to lock it in ASAP to take advantage of her publishing timelines."

"Yeah. I know." Jordan grew quiet again. Apparently, his silence appeared suspicious to Anderson. He could feel him looking at him through his periphery.

"And?" his friend asked.

"What?" Jordan said.

"Man. I've known you way too long. What's going on?"

"Nah. Nothing. It's just that…you know." Jordan was purposely beating around the bush.

"Spit it out!"

Jordan laughed. "We had a few drinks after the awards dinner. Then she invited me up to her penthouse."

"What!" Anderson's eyes widened. His foot hit the brake and the car behind them blared its horn. "Sorry." Anderson held up his hand to the driver. "Don't tell me you…"

"No!"

"Whoa! I was going to say that's not even like you. That's something *I* would have done," he admitted. Both Anderson and Jordan laughed.

"So, what happened?"

"None of that. We talked, exchanged a few kisses. Then I left. Now I'm home."

"What the—" Anderson shook his head. "You're trying to make me crash! So, what's next?"

"Nothing!"

"Nothing! You're losing your touch, man."

"I don't even have her number. I had to DM her to let her know it was cool hanging with her."

"You've been out of the game way too long, dude. Do you need a refresher course on women?"

"From you? Ha! Hell, no. I'm just chilling. I don't want her to feel pressured while we're trying to work out this deal. I'd hate for her to think she'd have to sleep with me to move things forward. We have to be careful."

"Okay, okay. You're right. So, wait until after everything is done and go for it after that." Anderson shook his head. "I have to admit…that girl is gorgeous!"

"She definitely is. And she seems cool, but I've seen sides of her that I'm still not so sure about."

"I get that," Anderson said as he maneuvered the car into a parking lot on Ventura Boulevard. "Let's go make this next deal happen, bruh!"

"Yeah, let's do it," Jordan said. They exited the car and headed to a lunch meeting with another network.

As a team, they handled business as usual but Jordan still couldn't keep his mind from traveling to thoughts of Ivy. Parts of her were still a mystery that he wanted to unravel.

Thirteen

Ivy was startled awake by the banging at her front door. Yawning, she sat up and blinked at her cell phone until the numbers came into focus. She'd missed several calls and texts.

"Oh, no!" Ivy threw the covers back and jumped out of the bed. She was late. No. She was *more* than late. Ivy was supposed to meet her mother, Lydia, and her sisters-in-law—Zoe, as well as Phoenix and Lincoln's wife, Britney—for brunch over two hours ago. She'd overslept again. Their monthly outing was Lydia's idea to keep the women of the Blackwell family connected. No husbands, brothers or children allowed. It was their time to eat and shop.

Lydia was going to have a few choice words for Ivy. Last month, Ivy hadn't made it because she was traveling for a conference. Her mom wasn't happy about that but understood that it was business. Ivy put one leg into her lounge pants and hopped to the door. She could hear Phoenix and Zoe on the other side. She pulled the door open and slapped her hand across her forehead.

"I'm so sorry!"

Zoe and Phoenix looked at Ivy, before looking at each other, shaking their heads and laughing. It wasn't them she had to worry about. Ivy stepped aside and waved Zoe and Phoenix into her sunlit foyer. Ivy looked past them and caught the irritated look in her mother's eye as she marched up the walk with Britney at her side.

"We brought you brunch. You'll want to eat fast so we can get to the stores. You know shopping calms your mother's nerves." Zoe held up a bag from the restaurant, kissed Ivy's cheek and then made her way to the kitchen to set the bag down.

Phoenix hugged Ivy. "How are you doing?"

Ivy huffed and shrugged.

"I know," Phoenix said. She headed to the kitchen behind Zoe. That was the designated meeting spot in Ivy's home when the girls got together.

"You haven't even showered?" Lydia's voice rang through Ivy's two-story foyer, laced with irritation.

"Hi, Mom."

Lydia stood planted in the doorway blinking at her daughter.

"Hey, Ivy," Britney said as she hugged Ivy and went off to the kitchen with the other girls.

Ivy knew they were getting out of the way of Lydia's annoyance. Despite the scowl she sported, Lydia looked stunning as always. Several weeks ago, she shocked everyone by shaving one side of her hair and cutting her long hair into a stylish one-sided bob. No one ever guessed that Lydia was in her sixties. Now with her new hairstyle, designer bag, mocha sweater dress and matching boots, Lydia looked even younger, despite her salt-and-pepper tresses. It almost looked as if she'd colored her hair that way.

With arms folded across her chest, Lydia glared at Ivy. She felt herself shrinking inside her mother's glare, but she shook that off with a groan.

"I'm sorry, Ma! I overslept."

Lydia finally stepped all the way in and pushed the door hard behind her. "And you look like you just dragged yourself from under your bed. Your eyes are dark and baggy. You're overextending yourself, and for the life of me, I can't understand why. You want for nothing!"

"That's not the point, Mom!" Ivy locked the door behind them.

"Then what is?" Lydia folded her arms again. She cocked her head to the side and demanded a response with her stern expression.

Ivy closed her eyes and inhaled.

"I like what I do, Ma. Not to mention it's benefitting the company."

"Oh, yeah? What about Dale Billington?"

Ivy looked away, trying to contain her frustration. Her parents wouldn't let her live that down. "I'm working on that," she said. Lydia raised her brow but held her rigid stance. "Wine?" Ivy asked but didn't stick around for an answer. She walked off toward the kitchen, got a bottle of her mother's favorite red. She poured her a glass, then set it on the massive marble island. "Let me go freshen up before I eat my breakfast."

"Go right ahead," Britney said.

"Yes! 'Cause I can smell you from here," Zoe said and laughed. Phoenix and Britney snickered. Lydia's face was stoic. The girls looked at the older woman and then each other before stifling their laughs.

It was obvious that Ivy and Zoe were closer than the others. They were similar in so many ways and they worked together daily at Blackwell since Ivy joined the team after Carter left to start his business.

Ivy playfully rolled her eyes and dismissed Zoe's jest with a wave. "Maybe I won't brush my teeth and then I can sit next to you in the car and talk all the way."

Phoenix and Britney fell out laughing.

"Don't encourage her," Zoe said, laughing too. "She just might do that."

"Oh! Hurry. We're already late," Lydia huffed, taking a place at the island before sipping her wine. "And put some cream under those eyes. You look like a raccoon."

"Oh, thanks, Ma!" Ivy said in a feigned cheerfulness. Arguing with her mother wouldn't be worth it. They were already on rocky terms.

Ivy dressed in record time and returned to the kitchen with the rest of the ladies. She was glad to hear her mother laughing along with the others when she stepped back in the room. Hopefully Lydia's annoyed state had dissipated.

"It took you long enough," Lydia said but complimented her on the cashmere sweater, jeans and knee-high boots she'd changed into. "Your eyes still look tired."

"Because I *am* tired, Mom." Ivy was becoming exasperated.

"I told you that you need to slow down. I don't know how else to say it."

"And, Mother, I told you I can handle it."

"Really? This is the third time this week you overslept. That's not like you. What time did you get to the office yesterday?" Lydia stood from the stool at the island and parked her hands on her hips.

Ivy simply averted her eyes.

"Exactly. Lately you're either late or missing stuff altogether. We called you at least ten times while we were at the restaurant. Did you even hear your phone ring? You fell asleep in church last Sunday. In fact, any time we sit still for more than five minutes you start yawning. Those bags around your eyes are becoming relentless. And don't think it's just me that notices all of this." Lydia looked from Phoenix to Zoe to Britney.

The girls tilted their heads, each giving a look showing their confirmation and compassion. Lydia was right.

"Every one of us has expressed concern about your well-being these past few weeks. Every time someone says something to you, you brush us off or get irritated. Next thing you know, we'll be visiting you in the hospital because of the toll this is taking on you." Lydia shook her head in frustration.

"I'm fine. I just have to get past a few deadlines. That's all."

"Listen." Her mother stepped over to Ivy and gently lifted her chin. "We're worried about you. We can get over missed brunches and your apparent lack of focus at times, but you've taken on too much and refuse to listen to anyone when we try to tell you to take a break. By all means, enjoy life, live your dreams, but don't let them take you out."

Ivy felt a tear threaten to trickle down her face. She blinked fast, moved away from the girls and headed to the fridge to grab a bottle of water. "I said I'll be fine."

"Oh, honey!" Lydia wrapped her arms around Ivy. "I'd recognize that stubbornness anywhere. You got it from me."

Ivy received her mother's embrace. It had been a long time since she felt it. She pulled back from her mother, looked at the others, then spoke. "Can we be done with the 'Let's pick on Ivy' session and just go shopping now?"

"See. That's the irritability we were talking about. Come on, Groucho, let's go buy something nice," Zoe said, which made everyone chuckle.

"Maybe we can find her a nice man while we're out shopping," Lydia smarted.

"Mom!"

"Well, if you would settle down I wouldn't have to worry about you so much. Live a little. You plan on being single all your life?"

"Don't start that again, Mom. Please!" Ivy's singleness wasn't by choice. She didn't have the strength needed for this conversation with her mother.

"All right! Okay!" Lydia waved dismissively and then winked at Zoe, Phoenix and Britney.

Ivy narrowed her eyes at Zoe and all the girls laughed.

"I'm not driving either," Ivy said. "I'm too tired." Her commend dripped with sarcasm.

Lydia furrowed her brow at Ivy. The others snickered.

The women stepped down from their stools at the kitchen island and started toward the door. Lydia led the line. Zoe hung back waiting for Ivy to lock up while the others headed to Britney's luxury SUV.

"Ivy," Zoe called her name quietly. "Did you see this?" Her sister-in-law held her phone up so Ivy could see. One of the social media gossip sites posted side-by-side images of Ivy and Kenya Brown with the headline about Kenya calling her a pretentious bitch.

Ivy drew in a sharp breath and blew it out with a groan. She felt her face grow warm. "How did this get out?"

"I'm sure she's responsible. This is probably why she picked a fight with you in the first place. I think what Jess said is true. This woman is using you to gain fame."

Ivy held her hands up. "What does she think? We're in some reality show?"

"Let's have the agency deal with it," Zoe suggested. "I just wanted to make sure you saw it before anyone came asking about it. Let's go enjoy what's left of our Blackwell ladies day out."

"Thanks. I hope no one comes asking. This is embarrassing." Most of all, Ivy hoped no one else in her family would see the post.

Britney tooted the horn.

"We're coming!" Ivy yelled as she and Zoe picked up their pace toward the car.

Inside the car, the conversation between the women was lively. Ivy would occasionally nod absently, smile or fling a quick comment into the conversation. Her mind was far away from what was going on as she settled into her own thoughts while watching the leaves begin to change on the trees as they drove by. She noticed Zoe watching her a few times. She probably figured Ivy was concerned about the social media post she'd just shown her but so much more weighed heavily on her mind, including her mother's words.

Despite "having it all," Ivy had goals she wanted to accomplish on her own. Yes. She was tired a lot. But it wouldn't always be that way. She'd be able to take a break soon enough and promised to schedule some time off right after the first leg of her book tour.

But if she was completely honest, the emotional toll was also part of the cause of her irritability. Her family was close. They were her anchor. But now her father was angry with her. Her mother was always on her back about slowing down and doing better at work. Whenever Ivy did slow down, she was reminded that despite the love of her family, she was lonely. She blamed herself for always pushing her boyfriends away with her ambition.

Lydia constantly reminded Ivy of her single status. Did she think Ivy chose to be single? She was the only one left out of her brothers that couldn't seem to manage a relationship for more than a few months. She wasn't trying to be the ultimate bachelorette. Even Carter was married now. He was the brother they all thought would be single forever.

Ivy desperately wanted to have success beyond what her parents had laid out for her. She needed to have something of her own, like her brothers. That didn't make her less proud to be a Blackwell. Why couldn't she have had love and success at the same time? Wasn't that possible?

Ivy's mind drifted to all the texts, emails and callbacks that were piling up. She still hadn't responded to Jordan's direct message because, to be frank, she wasn't sure what to say. That kiss still had her reeling. Dating him wouldn't be a good look since they could end up working together. Never could she have been accused of dating her way into an opportunity, or worse, sleeping her way to the top. And the show...

This would be a reality show. Would it bring more negative attention like the kind she was getting because of Kenya Brown? If so, she didn't want to be associated with anything like that.

But there was something about Jordan that she liked. Yes. He was smart and successful but something about his presence heightened all of her senses. She felt him in the room before she saw him enter. He was more than sexy. Something undeniable and combustible resided between them.

Ivy welcomed the idea of getting to know Jordan better despite a rocky start. She wanted to find out what made him tick. Jordan didn't seem put off by her busy schedule. He had one himself. It's just that the timing wasn't right at all. How could she fit him into her life? She'd probably push Jordan away like she had with other men she dated. With all that she had going on, Ivy didn't even have the emotional capacity to deal with a man. She wanted to respond to Jordan. Ivy thought of him often—especially the kiss they shared—but she needed more time.

After the tour, she promised to take a little time off. And after she found out about the show, maybe she would consider kissing Jordan Chambers again.

Fourteen

Jordan arrived at his office earlier than usual in preparation for the meeting with his team, Ivy's and the network that had accepted his pitch for the show. From this point forward, he'd wanted to keep all communications between him and the Money Maven professional and cordial. But that didn't stop him from looking forward to seeing her at their upcoming meeting.

Jordan had gotten the message loud and clear that she wasn't interested in anything more. Weeks had passed since he'd last seen or heard from Ivy. To date, she'd never responded to his DM. All communication between them went through their teams. Contracts had been reviewed on all sides and now it was time to talk about their production schedule. If he wanted to pursue anything further with Ivy, it would have to wait.

Jordan took special care in preparing for the meeting, not just professionally, but personally. He was meticulous in choosing his outfit, a stylish sweater, dress pants and designer shoes. This was way dressier that he'd normally wear to the office but he was going to see Ivy today. Jordan couldn't half-step. He added a light spray of his favorite cologne. The scent was fresh and clean. Jordan wanted the fact that he would be around Ivy to be no big deal. Yet he anticipated her arrival with every part of his being. The truth was, before he ever put his lips on Ivy, she'd already intrigued him. If anything, he would follow her lead. There was more to know about Ivy Blackwell. Their time together in New York had only allowed him to touch the surface.

Jordan looked at his watch once more. The meeting was scheduled to start soon, though not soon enough as far as he was concerned. He wondered how Ivy would respond to seeing him. Just then, he thought about how large her following was. It was possible that she'd never even seen his message. Perhaps it was buried in a sea of hundreds of other DMs? In that moment a wave of hoped passed through him. He'd rather she had not seen the message at all than to see it and ignore it.

Burying himself in his work, Jordan was startled when the office assistant knocked and then peeked her head inside his office.

"Ms. Blackwell and her team have arrived and the network will be up shortly."

"Thank you, Kayla."

Ivy was in the building. A smile spread across his face as he closed out the programs on his laptop and shut it down.

He caught up with Anderson on the way to the conference room. He spotted Ivy through the glass wall and felt a tightening in his stomach. Once inside, it was all business. Jordan and his team greeting everyone with a firm handshake and a professional demeanor.

"Ms. Blackwell." Jordan nodded cordially when he greeted her.

"Great to see you again, Mr. Chambers," she responded with a tight smile, receiving his firm handshake and returning just the right amount of firmness.

Jordan tried to be discreet. His gaze swept over Ivy quickly. He never imagined a woman could look so sexy in a suit. His eyes made their way to her lips. He remembered how soft they felt when they kissed. He remembered the fire that ignited in his belly when her lips met his. He pulled himself together.

"Let's get started." Jordan clasped his hands together before sitting at the head of the conference table.

They got right down to business. Within the hour, they'd determined a full schedule of dates for picking show participants, studios, filming, postproduction and promos. Input from the network included having all show participants be celebrities with terrible spending habits. The show, titled *Fix My Finances*, would be filmed in LA over a four-week period. The pilot season would consist of six episodes. Ivy asked plenty of good questions. It was obvious she wasn't privy to the world of television. All they needed now was confirmation from the studio and other partners to make sure the schedule would work with everyone involved.

By the end of the meeting, Ivy smiled, but that smile didn't reach her eyes. Jordan wasn't sure what had happened since he'd last spoken to her after that awards ceremony. He thought she was excited about the show. What changed?

As everyone filed out of the conference room, Jordan called Ivy's name.

At first, he studied her when she turned to him. He couldn't read her expression. Again, he wondered if she'd seen his message.

"Just wondering about your thoughts after today. Are you still excited?" he asked.

"Of course," Ivy said, but didn't sound convincing. Her demeanor seemed rigid.

Jordan studied her another moment. She averted her eyes.

"Who wouldn't be excited?" she reiterated, looking toward the door.

"Am I...holding you up?" Jordan scrunched his brows as he asked.

"Um. No! I do have to get ready for a book signing this evening. I just got in early this morning and I'm a bit tired. Jet lag setting in already. That's all." Ivy shifted her weight from one foot to the other. "My schedule is booked solid while I'm here in LA. But... as for the show—yes, I'm excited. I just have to work out some things on my end schedule-wise. Know what I mean?"

He narrowed his eyes at Ivy. Something was off with her. She didn't seem the same. The spark was gone. Perhaps she didn't want to be bothered with him. Or maybe now that it was confirmed that they would be working together, she felt awkward about the kiss they shared. Maybe she was fighting her feelings just like he was.

Dear Reader,

I am writing to announce the launch of a huge **FREE BOOK GIVEAWAY**... and to let you know that YOU are entitled to choose up to FOUR fantastic books that WE pay for.

Try **Harlequin® Desire** books featuring the worlds of the American elite with juicy plot twists, delicious sensuality and intriguing scandal.

Try **Harlequin Presents® Larger-Print** books featuring the glamourous lives of royals and billionaires in a world of exotic locations, where passion knows no bounds.

Or **TRY BOTH!**

In return, we ask just one favor: Would you please participate in our brief Reader Survey? We'd love to hear from you.

This FREE BOOKS GIVEAWAY means that your introductory shipment is completely free, even the shipping! If you decide to continue, you can look forward to curated monthly shipments of brand-new books from your selected series, always at a discount off the cover price! Plus you can cancel any time. Who could pass up a deal like that?

Sincerely

Pam Powers

Pam Powers
For Harlequin Reader Service

Complete the survey below and return it today to receive up to 4 FREE BOOKS and FREE GIFTS guaranteed!

FREE BOOKS GIVEAWAY
Reader Survey

1

Do you prefer stories with happy endings?

◯ YES   ◯ NO

2

Do you share your favorite books with friends?

◯ YES   ◯ NO

3

Do you often choose to read instead of watching TV?

◯ YES   ◯ NO

YES! Please send me my Free Rewards, consisting of **2 Free Books from each series I select** and **Free Mystery Gifts**. I understand that I am under no obligation to buy anything, no purchase necessary see terms and conditions for details.

❏ **Harlequin Desire®** (225/326 HDL GRLR)
❏ **Harlequin Presents® Larger-Print** (176/376 HDL GRLR)
❏ **Try Both** (225/326 & 176/376 HDL GRL3)

FIRST NAME   LAST NAME

ADDRESS

APT.#   CITY

STATE/PROV.   ZIP/POSTAL CODE

EMAIL ❏ Please check this box if you would like to receive newsletters and promotional emails from Harlequin Enterprises ULC and its affiliates. You can unsubscribe anytime.

HD/HP-122-FBG22_HD-HP-122-FBGVR

Jordan looked around to make sure no one was in earshot before speaking. He spoke softly. "I hope you don't feel awkward about—"

"No!" she interrupted. Her tone was sharp and louder than expected. She looked around before saying in a lower tone, "I'm fine. This is a professional relationship now."

Jordan held his hands up. "Yes, it is. I look forward to working with you." He straightened his back. He felt coolness emanating from her but nevertheless he had to feel her out.

Ivy offered another tight smile and nodded. "Me too."

"Is everything okay with us?" he asked outright.

"Yes. It's fine. Really. I just have a lot going on." Ivy seemed sincere when she said that.

Jordan felt a bit relieved.

"Your signing this evening. Where is it? Maybe some of us can come support you—perhaps get a few photos of you signing books. We could use it for the show."

"Oh. Sure. Good idea! It's a great bookstore that's been around for years. They get a lot of bookings for big signings. My publicist thought it would be a good place to do a signing while I was here. I'll send you the address."

"Good. Text it to me," Jordan said.

Ivy hesitated for a moment. "Sure." She pulled out her phone. "What's your number?"

Once he gave it to her, she sent the link.

Jordan tapped on it and studied the information. "I know this store. We've filmed there a few times."

"Great." Ivy covered an elongated yawn.

"Sorry to be such a bore," Jordan teased.

That got a chuckle out of her. "I'm sorry. I'd better get going."

"Good luck with the signing. I'll see you there. Maybe…" Jordan was about to say they could go for a drink after but decided to keep his suggestion to himself. "I'll get a copy for my mother."

"I'll make sure to put in a special message for her." Her smile seemed genuine to Jordan for the first time since the meeting started.

"That would be nice. Thanks."

"See you later," Ivy said and turned to leave without waiting for his response.

Jordan wasn't sure what has just happened but he was glad that he'd get to see her again at the bookstore.

Back in his office, he put his head down and got deep into his work. Later he shared the fact that Ivy would be signing at the bookstore. Unfortunately, Anderson couldn't make it. His assistant, Kayla, had a family dinner. Jordan decided to attend alone and take a few pictures on his cell phone. They'd have more chances to get footage of Ivy for the show promos.

He went home to freshen up before going over to the book signing. Again, he took meticulous care in his attire and chosen scent. He arrived right on time. The line was snaked outside the store and down the block. He hadn't expected so many people. How was she going to sign books for all these people in an hour? He pressed his way inside and searched for the owner. There was no way he was standing in that line. There had to be at least a hundred people waiting to see her. Jordan was impressed.

The owner, a short, gray-haired woman named Pat, greeted him with a big hug and warm smile.

"You here to see the Money Maven?" She let out a big laugh. "She's a looker. Isn't she?"

"Actually, yes. And she is quite beautiful. We're working with her."

"Oh, good! How exciting!" She clapped her hands together. "Follow me. I'll take you to her."

Pat grabbed Jordan's hand and navigated through the crowd until she was at Ivy's side. "Ms. Blackwell. You have company."

Ivy looked up at the older woman. "Thanks, Pat."

"No problem. And I'll have someone bring you some more water."

She nodded appreciatively, then turned toward Jordan after Pat hurried off. "Hi," Ivy said. She smiled, but again, it didn't reach her tired eyes.

Jordan empathized with her. He knew what it was like to feel as though he were running on fumes.

"Hey!" he said back. "Nice crowd." He looked around again, seeing nothing but heads over the shelves. "Do your thing. Mind if I take a few pictures while you're signing?"

"No problem," Ivy said.

Jordan stepped out of the way. He took pictures of Ivy scribbling her signature in each book and caught a few shots of the enthused crowd.

Ivy's agent and publisher flanked her on both sides, opening books to the title pages and placing sticky notes with people's names inside. Jordan captured all of that. Then he stuck around until the end of the signing, which was well beyond an hour by the time they cut the line off. Had they allowed people to keep coming, Ivy would have been in the bookstore beyond closing.

When she was done, Pat had her sign a few extra copies and told her she would put stickers on those books to let people know they had been autographed by her.

Once they cleared out all the people, Ivy stood, stretched and yawned.

"I'll get us a car," she told her female companions.

"How far are you going?" Jordan asked.

"The Four Seasons," Ivy said.

"No need to get a car. I'll take you."

"You have room for all three of us?" Ivy asked in surprise.

"Yep."

"That's awesome. Thanks so much, Jordan!" Ivy said. "I can't wait to get to my bed."

Ivy's mention of her bed made him chuckle on the inside. Jordan knew she was tired but wished he could share a few moments with her like they had before. He really wanted to know what was going on with her and make sure she wasn't feeling awkward about what had happened between them.

"It would be my pleasure. You ladies look like you can't get to your hotel fast enough. I know how those New York to LA flights get to you."

"You're right," one of the girls said. "I know you're tired, Ivy, but we want to hang out at the hotel bar. If you feel up to it after getting some rest, join us."

"I'll probably see you ladies in the morning," Ivy said. "Before we adjust to this time difference, we'll be in another time zone. I'm going to get my rest."

Jordan drove them the short distance to the hotel.

Though it took no more than a few minutes, Jordan had to nudge Ivy awake once they arrived.

Jordan exited the car. The hotel attendants helped the ladies out. They said their goodbyes and headed inside. Ivy took her time getting out of the car. Jordan took her by the arm to help steady her.

"I'm going to go ahead and walk her to the room," he said to the attendant. He nodded in return.

"No, Jordan. You don't have to do that. I'll be fine," Ivy insisted, yawning yet again.

"I want to make sure you're okay," Jordan said.

Ivy let her hands flop to her sides and sighed. "Fine." She'd given up her resistance.

Jordan walked Ivy through the lavish lobby toward the elevators.

She stopped abruptly and turned to him. "Listen. Don't think you're going to come to my room and try to pick up where you left off in New York. I should never have kissed you."

Jordan's jaw clenched. He couldn't believe she was accusing him of having ulterior motives. He was just genuinely concerned about her well-being. "That wasn't my intention."

"I just wanted to be clear." Ivy's hands were on her hips.

Jordan reared his head back. "What kind of person… You know what? Never mind! I was just trying to be nice. Have a good night." Jordan's words were curt. He backed away.

"Whatever!" Ivy said and folded her arms across her chest.

Jordan glowered at her. He was going to say more,

like tell her she was being unreasonable. But then thought better of it. Maybe he'd sent mixed messages. Perhaps Hollywood's bad rap on the treatment of women was to blame. He wasn't sure, but it didn't take much for him to recognize when his presence wasn't welcomed.

At one last gesture prompted by his chivalrous nature, Jordan put distance between them but waited until the elevator came. At least he would know she made it onto the elevator safely. As the doors opened, Ivy looked back at him. Her irritated glare melted. Her eyes lost the rest of their spark and she seemed to look past him. Then Ivy swooned, and a moment later she crumpled to the floor. Jordan's heart fell into his stomach and he heard himself yell Ivy's name.

Fifteen

Ivy blinked. Blinding brightness caused her to shut her eyes immediately. She squeezed them tight and tried to open them again. This time, she lifted her heavy lids slowly. For a moment she wondered where she was. Beeping machines grounded her. Was this a hospital? Ivy blinked a few times again. Faded memories tried to come to her but only showed flashes.

Why was she here? she wondered. Was she in New York? Where was her family?

"Ivy," someone said her name. They sounded relieved.

The person sounded familiar but she couldn't figure out who it was. She lifted herself up in the bed, trying to focus on the bright room around her. Her sight was blurry but her ears seem to hear more keenly. Those beeping sounds came in loudest. She heard voices in the distance. There were footsteps.

"Nurse! She's awake," the familiar voice said. After a few padded steps, someone stood before her. "Ivy. Can you hear me?"

Ivy looked up. Clarity rolled in pushing the haze away. "Jordan?" Her voice was hoarse. She cleared her throat. "W-what are you doing here?" She looked around again, taking in the emergency room. "Why am *I* here?"

"You fainted," Jordan said and gently touched her hand. His hand felt good on hers. She needed to feel his warmth. Ivy looked down at it. He followed her eyes and moved his hand away. "Sorry," he said before asking, "How are you feeling?"

"I'm okay. You said I fainted? Where?"

"At the hotel, just before getting into the elevator," he told her. "I tried to get in touch with your agent and the other woman you were with, but couldn't get into your phone. I called 911 and got you here ASAP."

She asked anxiously, "Did you tell anyone else?"

"I didn't know who else to call. I reached out to your cousin Tyler through his Instagram, but I haven't heard anything back. I don't have his phone number."

Ivy tried to sit up fast. Her head hurt. Slowly she sat back. "What did you say to him?"

"I didn't want to alarm him, so I just said to call me and left my number."

"How long have I been in here?" She looked at the IV connected to her arm.

"About two hours. The doctors ran some tests. I didn't want you to wake up alone." Jordan walked over to the chair he was sitting in. "Here's your phone. I was hoping someone would call that could get me closer to one of your family members."

"No!" Ivy held both hands up. Jordan's brows furrowed. "I mean…thanks. I don't want to alarm anyone without knowing what's happening."

"Okay. I'll let the nurse know you're awake." He handed her cell phone to her. "Now you can call who you need to." Jordan stepped out, giving her space to think about what was happening.

Everything was getting clearer. She remembered being in the hotel, exchanging words with Jordan. Ivy cringed. She recalled that they may not have been nice words. But what caused her to faint?

She laid back on the cool pillows. Now that she thought about it, she had a pretty good idea of what caused her to faint. Ivy had been going nonstop all week. Today was by far the most taxing day of them all. Starting with an extremely early flight, the meeting with Jordan's production company, followed by an interview at a radio station. A mini–photo session to capture pictures and footage of what was happening behind the scenes on her trip to LA and the book tour in general. The last thing was her book signing. She hadn't had a solid meal and was tired beyond any kind of fatigue she'd ever felt.

Ivy closed her eyes and a tear spilled from her eye down the side of her face. She was glad Jordan wasn't able to get into her phone to call anyone. Especially Lydia. The last thing she needed to hear from her mom was "I told you so." She needed to find out what exactly was wrong with her before she spoke with her family.

Jordan stuck around so someone could be here when she opened her eyes. If she remembered correctly, she had been pretty awful to him, which made his gesture to be there for her even more admirable. Ivy sighed. She'd clearly bitten off way more than she could chew, but what could she do about it now?

"Ms. Blackwell!" An older distinguished-looking gentleman pushed the curtain aside and stepped in closer to her bed. "It's good to see you awake. How are you feeling?"

"Okay, I guess. Slight headache." Ivy narrowed her eyes to see the name written across the doctor's white coat. "Dr…"

"Brighton," he said for her.

Ivy pulled herself into a sitting position and rested her back against the bed. "What happened to me?"

"The good news is that it doesn't look like anything major such as a heart attack." He flipped through a chart he had secured on a clipboard. "Your EKG came out fine." He ran down a list of other tests. "I believe your passing out was your body's response to unchecked stress."

"How would you know that?"

"Well, the body gives lots of clues when we're stressed. The problem is that we often overlook the symptoms or consider them to be signs of other things."

"Like what?"

"Well, things as simple as hair shedding or loss."

"Hair loss?"

"That's right. You may notice more hair coming out in your combs than usual. Other symptoms include irritability, loss of focus, headaches, fatigue, muscle stiffness in the back or neck, sleeplessness… The list goes on. Right now, all signs are pointing to stress. But if you don't slow down, you're going to have some bigger issues to contend with. I'm prescribing rest and would suggest you clear your calendar for the next few days."

"The next few days!" Ivy sat up straighter and her posture became rigid. "Doctor, I'm in the middle of a book tour. I have to be in San Francisco by…" She looked at her wrist. Her watch wasn't there. "What day is it?"

"It's still Wednesday for another few minutes."

"Tomorrow evening. I have a signing tomorrow and another one the day after that." Ivy didn't mention all the media opportunities she'd committed to in each city, including radio interviews, news segments and talk show appearances that were scheduled for each city. Not to mention all the mini shoots to get B-roll footage at major landmarks in each location.

"For the sake of your health, I strongly suggest you reschedule. I don't think those bookstores are going anywhere. Now," Dr. Brighton said with finality as if he were her father. "We're waiting on one last test but would like to keep you overnight for observation."

"Overnight! I can't do that." Ivy slumped down and groaned.

Dr. Brighton sighed and pressed his lips together. "And I can't make you, but I'd hate to see you hospitalized again with more serious issues, but that's exactly what is going to happen if you don't take care of yourself now. Your body needs this, Ms. Blackwell. Please think about it seriously." The doctor raised a brow and looked at her as if he were waiting on her to make the right decision. "I'll go check on that other test."

The moment Dr. Brighton stepped out of her bay, Ivy put her face in her hands and cried. She knew he was right. Over the past few weeks, she'd exhibited every single symptom that he'd mentioned as signs of stress. Her life had become a runaway train that she couldn't seem to slow down. And now that she had the show, everything was taking off at the same time. She was tired but so happy with all of her progress. The key words were *her progress*. She had made all of this happen. These were *her* accomplishments.

Ivy sighed. She just needed to pace herself and then things would fall into place. The other thing she had to do was keep this little mishap away from her family. They couldn't know about her hospitalization. Because if they got wind of it, all hell would break loose. She released a relieved breath. She hated ending up in the ER, but she was thankful this hadn't happened when she was in New York.

"You're okay?" Jordan said softly, coming back into the room.

"Yeah." Her quick response was a whisper. "I'm fine." Ivy swatted her tears away. She didn't want to cry in front of Jordan. "Look, um, I think I remember not being very nice to you before all of this."

"Don't worry about it."

She held one hand up, making him pause. "I need to apologize and ask you two questions."

"Sure. Anything."

Ivy swallowed. "I know this is a lot to ask." She paused. "It's okay. Ask me whatever you need."

Ivy shut her eyes for a moment. She lifted her head toward the ceiling before looking straight at Jordan. She took another breath before asking, "Can you keep this little situation between the two of us?" She sank into her shoulders and pleaded with a puppy dog look. Ivy could summarize the questions behind Jordan's surprised expression. Eventually she'd explain to him why, but not now.

"And the other question?" Jordan looked as if he wasn't sure he wanted to hear the second one.

"Can you stay?"

Sixteen

Jordan was exhausted. He'd stayed with Ivy until the hospital placed her in a room, and refused to leave until he was sure that she was resting peacefully. That relaxed sleep finally came after four in the morning with the help of a sleeping aid. That gave him and Ivy plenty of time to talk.

When she felt more comfortable, she explained why she didn't want anyone to contact her family. A chorus of "I told you so" from them was the last thing she needed. Jordan insisted that she had to tell them at some point and finally she promised once the tour was over.

He had left the hospital, promising Ivy that he'd return that afternoon and then texted Anderson to let him know that he'd be in the office late. Jordan needed time to rest his body, and wrestle with the burgeoning feelings that were coming up for Ivy. She apologized for her attitude several times throughout the night.

Fortunately, it was a light day at the office. Jordan visited the set to check one of the shows in production. Things were looking up for his company. Not only did the network approve Ivy's show, a few other ideas were also in the works. Content was in demand so they had to stay on their toes, keep fresh ideas coming and keep delivering.

Jordan's phone vibrated while he was in the studio. He looked at the caller, excused himself and headed outside to answer so he wouldn't disturb the actors.

"Hey! How are you feeling?" he asked Ivy.

"Better now that I got some rest."

Jordan looked at his watch—it was almost quitting time. "How long have you been up?"

"A few hours. I made some calls, had my agent reschedule my signings for the next few days." Ivy quieted a moment. "They're letting me out of here."

"Do you need me to come and get you?"

Jordan heard her sigh. "I really don't want to be a burden."

"So, what are you going to do, call a ride share company? Give me a half hour." Jordan didn't hesitate. Back inside, he let the crew know he was heading out.

When he arrived at the hospital, Ivy was dressed and ready to go. He could tell that she'd tried to finger comb her disheveled hair. Her eyes still looked tired. Jordan had now seen her in several states—formal gowns with a face full of makeup, leggings and hoodies and now a worn post-hospital-stay look. And each and every time, she was simply beautiful in his eyes.

Trying to be a gentleman, Jordan escorted her from the hospital to her hotel suite. She'd extended her stay until her next signing in two days. The rest of the crew flew back to New York and would meet her at the East Coast book tour dates. He made sure she was comfortable before attempting to leave. Even though a huge part of him wanted to stay. But in any event, it became important to him to make sure she was all right.

"So…" Jordan stuffed a hand in his jeans pocket. "You're all good?"

"Yes. Thanks." Ivy still moved a bit slow. She walked over to the refrigerator, opened a bottled water and took a long sip. "I just need a long, hot shower."

"Okay. Let me know if you need anything." He looked into her eyes. Suddenly he wanted to be needed by her.

"I will." She smiled. It was the sweetest smile he'd ever seen on a woman. "Thanks again…for everything." She put her bottle of water aside and leaned against the wall, arms folded, with her eyes on him.

"Do you have something to eat for later so you don't have to go out?" He was finding reasons to stay or have to come back. Right or wrong, Jordan wanted to be by her side.

"I'll probably order room service. I won't bother you again, I promise."

"No. It's no bother at all," he insisted, wondering yet again why he was so drawn to Ivy. They shared totally different backgrounds but had so much in common. Both worked too hard and spent too much time alone. Despite not knowing Ivy for very long, he found comfort in her presence, even when she was being irritable most of that time. Jordan stepped toward the door. He was close enough to reach for the knob. He remembered their kiss and instinctively licked his lips. "Okay, but if you need anything, I'm only a phone call away." He lifted his cell. Jordan was mastering the art of procrastination. He didn't move any closer to the door. Ivy hadn't moved either. They watched each other for a few moments.

"You're a good guy, Jordan Chambers, but don't worry about me. I just need rest. I can manage feeding myself and walking around this room."

"Just trying to be helpful." Jordan shrugged and tilted his head to the side.

"And I appreciate you." Her voice was soft. It flowed through him like a melody in the air.

They locked eyes again. The unspoken connection spoke volumes compared to what they had said with their mouths. Jordan didn't believe she wanted him to go.

"You want me to go now?" His voice was a bit huskier than he intended. He wanted her to tell him to stay.

Ivy didn't say anything.

Say no, Jordan said in his head. His body felt warm as if a sudden fever rose in him. He couldn't deny his wild attraction to Ivy. He noticed that she still hadn't said for him to go or stay. He knew she needed rest. Maybe he should go before she became irritable again. That would have reminded him to keep his distance. Who wanted to be with someone who was insufferable?

Ivy said that she wasn't usually the incessantly irritable type. Something inside him believed her. Even the doctor admitted that her attitude could have been a sign of her exhaustion. Besides, despite her delivery, he understood her position about drawing a line between them that night.

If they were going to be working together, getting intimate wouldn't necessarily be a good look for her. The double standardized world they lived in would give him credit and ridicule her. Having a relationship with the talent could *really* complicate things. Jordan had been there before. He knew he liked Ivy but was willing to wait until they could explore each other without the complexities that came with a working relationship.

Jordan worked out all the scenarios in his head. What if the show was a hit and they were asked to film additional seasons after the pilot? Maybe he would have to wait a little longer, but at some point, he wanted to explore more with Ivy Blackwell. Somehow, he knew she'd be worth the wait.

"Jordan." She called his name softly, pulling him from his thoughts. "I really wouldn't mind if you stayed. That's if you can. I don't want to impose."

"I can stay." Jordan wanted to pull her into his arms, but kept his composure. He looked at his watch as if he had someplace else he needed to be.

"If you did leave, I'd be all alone again." Ivy cast her eyes downward. When she looked back up at him, he felt his core tighten. For a brief moment, he saw the glimmer of loneliness in her eyes. It dissipated.

Jordan stepped farther into the room. "What about Tyler?"

"Tyler and Kendall are out of town. My team went back to New York. I'm here by myself and could use the company."

"At least I can make sure you have a good meal before you fall asleep tonight."

The smile that spread across Ivy's face seemed sweet but had a hint of spice in it.

"Great! Why don't you go and get it while I freshen up? I need to get the scent of the hospital off me."

"Preferences?"

"No hospital food." Both of them laughed.

"Allergies?" he asked.

"None. I really enjoy sushi, seafood, Italian…"

"Perfect! I'll be right back."

Jordan called into one of his favorite Italian restaurants and ordered an array of dishes. He also stopped for a bottle of scotch. By the time, he returned, Ivy was out of the shower and had slipped into another comfortable pair of leggings, a T-shirt and fluffy slippers. Again, she was absolutely beautiful. Jordan looked forward to spending the next few hours with her. For some reason, he couldn't get enough of her.

Seventeen

This was the second time Ivy had invited Jordan to her hotel room within a few short weeks. Why did she feel so comfortable around him? She did know. Yes, their first impressions were rocky as heck, but Jordan Chambers had certainly redeemed himself.

Ivy couldn't say she didn't think about their kiss often. Jordan's good looks had captured her attention from day one. She regretted that she hadn't been nice to him on more than on occasion, especially the times he hadn't spilled his drinks on her. Now she realized why she'd been so irritable all the time. That wasn't really her. The exhaustion made her insufferable.

She knew she was asking a lot when she asked him to stay with her at the hospital but she had absolutely no one else she could call on. She didn't have a personal relationship with her agent and publicists and the only other person that she was really close to within LA was out of town. She could have trusted Tyler to keep her secret had he been home.

Ivy felt incredibly alone but now Jordan was by her side.

Finding herself curled up on the couch again, she looked over at the half-eaten dishes strewn across the coffee table in her hotel suite. They had paused the comedy show they were watching because Jordan's phone rang. He had stepped away to take the call. At first, Ivy couldn't help wondering if it was another woman but then she remembered their conversation about being single. Relief washed over her. She definitely wasn't the type to deal with married men. Nor was she interested in being anyone's side chick. Heck! If she could be someone's chick, period, she might applaud herself. Her last three relationships were short-lived failures, mostly on her part. She was convinced that men just didn't understand her. Perhaps growing up as the only girl in a household full of boys impacted her more than she realized. She never felt like she needed a man, but she sure liked having one around.

What would it be like to date Jordan? Ivy entertained that thought for a moment. The first strike against them would be the fact that both of them traveled a lot. Second, they lived far from one another. She'd tried the long-distance thing before and it sucked horribly.

"Okay. I'll send you all the details when I book," she heard Jordan say as he walked back into the suite. He'd left the door cracked so he could get back in. "Love you too. Good night."

Ivy turned to him just as he ended the call. "Everything okay?"

"It will be." Jordan huffed. "Family stuff. That was my mom."

"Oh! Cool." She was glad to hear it was his mom. "I'm going to get this stuff out of our way." Ivy unfolded her legs from under her and put the leftover scraps in the trash. "A drink?"

"Sure."

"I want to taste this scotch you bought. Neat?"

"You know me," Jordan joked.

"I guess we both know more about each other than we would have imagined at this point," Ivy said softly.

"After that call, I could use something to take the edge off," he added.

"Coming right up!" Ivy took the bottle from the coffee table, grabbed two glasses and poured about an inch of scotch into each. The truth was she could also use something to help her unwind as well. Having Jordan around was great, but she couldn't keep her eyes off him. It wasn't like she hadn't caught him staring a few times either.

The sensual tension between them was extremely apparent. Being around him was like playing with matches. She'd already felt a spark inside her belly a time or two, like when he touched her hand at the hospital. She felt the warmth of care, but also something hotter. And then again, she remembered the feel of his lips on hers.

Ivy brought both glasses back to the living room area and placed them on the table. She sat back down, picked up the remote and pointed it at the television.

The paused comedian came back to life, right in the middle of a joke. Ivy was seated on one side of the sofa and Jordan on the other. Both of them guffawed hard at the man's jokes.

"You have no idea how much I love to laugh," Ivy said after catching her breath.

Jordan turned and looked at her. She felt as if he was looking into her soul. "Me too." He turned back to the television. That gave Ivy a moment to study his profile. His jawline was strong and sculptured. Smooth brown skin reminded her of warm, melted milk chocolate. And that dimple. Have mercy! Whenever he smiled or laughed, it played peekaboo, making her want to kiss the crevice. And his eyes radiated a sexy laziness and were framed by lush lashes most women would pay to have.

More laughter. The show was over too soon. "Let's watch something else," Ivy said quickly. She didn't want Jordan to leave. Yet she also didn't want too much idle time to pass between them. Otherwise, they'd be forced to reckon with the chemistry that sat in the room like a large pink elephant.

Jordan looked at his watch. "I'm up for it if you are."

"Do you have to go?" Ivy hoped he could stay.

"No. I just don't want to wear out my welcome. If you get tired, just let me know."

"Are you going to tuck me in?" Ivy froze after those words left her lips. She didn't mean to be so flirtatious. And she couldn't even blame it on the scotch since she'd barely touched her drink. Ivy felt Jordan looking at her. She could see him through her peripheral but couldn't tell if he was smiling or not. To distract herself, she picked up her glass and took a small sip. The liquid strolled down her throat like lava, leaving a savory burn in its wake. Finally, she heard him laughing.

"Are you flirting with me?"

With her glass to her lips, she turned toward him. "Maybe."

Jordan was definitely smiling. "Interesting," he said through perfect teeth.

Ivy put the glass down. "I read a room well and I'm pretty...how should I say this? Direct. I'm grateful for you keeping me company and being kind enough to be here for me, but I won't deny the fact that I find you attractive." She cleared her throat. "I just don't think it would be a good idea for us to become...entangled. Dating or sleeping with people that you do business with usually doesn't turn out well. At least, it hasn't worked out for me in the past. However, I'm glad you're here."

"Well, since we're being frank..." Jordan sat up and looked directly into Ivy's eyes. His expression was serious. "I thought you were stunning since the day I spilled wine on your beautiful dress at the wrap party. If I hadn't been working that night and didn't almost ruin your outfit, I would have asked for your number then. After the next spill, I figured I'd ruined my chances." He blew out a breath. "So, imagine my surprise when Anderson suggested we contact you regarding a show idea. I thought you were going to get up from the table and leave during that first meeting."

"Really?" She flashed him a teasing look. "Well, to be honest, the thought did cross my mind!"

"I bet. Well, in any event, I've wanted to know more about you ever since that first night. Needless to say, I find you extremely attractive whether you're wearing a gown, suit, leggings, hoodies, coffee or wine."

Ivy's laugher spilled from her mouth like a faucet. "Remind me to send you my cleaning bill."

Jordan chuckled too. Several moments ticked by with them simply taking each other in. Jordan moved closer to her on the couch. "Well, where does that put us, Ms. Blackwell?"

Ivy grinned. She tilted her head and asked seriously, "Where would you like it to?"

Jordan drew in a breath. "Right where we are. Exploring."

Ivy's expression turned serious. She looked down at her glass and placed it back on the table, wanting Jordan to understand that this was all her speaking, not the scotch. "I have an idea where I'd like for it to go, but I'm concerned about what happens next. I've never been good at casual dating and I'm not exactly fling material. Plus, I have a busy life. I just don't have the time to dedicate to giving situations like this what it needs."

"I get that. It's a risk I'm willing to take." Jordan moved even closer to her. "But tell me what you'd like." His voice was like a caress. "Be honest with me."

A sprig of warmth started in Ivy's belly and made goose bumps rise on her skin. She covered her lips with her hand and thought about how to muster the words. "Brutally honest?"

"Brutally," he repeated. "I promise you. I can take it."

"I want what's brewing here," Ivy said. She felt her voice grow hoarse with the weight of longing.

"Me too." Jordan was so close now that Ivy could feel his breath on her cheek.

"But what happens after that?" She felt deflated by the reality of her words.

Jordan gently touched her cheek, turning her face toward him. "I like you. I'm willing to take the chance and see how far this could go. I don't believe either of us got to where we are in our lives by playing it safe."

Jordan got that right. Everything about him made her want more. His words. His deep, husky voice. The heat emanating from him that seemed to transfer to her. Finally, her lips said, "One day at a time. No commitments." Her mind caught up only after the words were out. What had she just agreed to? An *anything goes* arrangement? Those could be just as dangerous.

"Just two consenting adults, with busy lives, enjoying each other's company," Jordan said. Ivy stared as each word fell from his full, luscious lips.

Giving in, she shrugged. "Having fun until it's no longer feeling like fun. Then a clean break. Nothing awkward or complicated. Deal?"

"Deal."

Ivy held up her pinkie. "Pinkie swear?"

Jordan threw his head back and laughed.

Ivy shrugged again. "It's less formal than a handshake but still binding."

"Fine." He linked his pinkie with hers. After, he looked into her eyes again, and Ivy felt his gaze penetrate her soul once again.

"Kiss me, Jordan," she whispered.

Without hesitation, Jordan pulled Ivy into his embrace and unleashed a passion so complete she was breathless within seconds. Ivy hugged him back, groping hungrily at his sweater. The kiss was frantic, urgent even. They ravished each other as if they were water quenching one another's thirst.

"I've been wanting to kiss you again since the day you left my room in New York," Ivy panted.

"And not one day has gone by without me thinking about kissing you again," Jordan admitted gruffly.

Ivy pulled him in for more. They kissed and kissed and kissed until both their bodies were on fire. Then they broke apart just long enough to breathe and start right back up again. Jordan's hands roamed Ivy's body and she explored all of his. Jordan's skin felt feverish under Ivy's touch. Soon she wouldn't be able to control her cravings. She had to make a decision. Either send him home or take him to her bedroom.

"You have protection?" she managed to gasp a whisper.

Jordan returned a breathy, "Yes." He pulled back for a moment and searched her face. "You sure about this?"

Instead of answering, Ivy stood, took him by the hand and led him to her room. She couldn't remember ever being this impulsive but was enjoying every moment of it.

Inside the room, Jordan took his time slowly peeling off each item of clothing and kissing the places the garments used to cover. He started with her T-shirt. Lifting it and kissing her belly. He unhooked her bra and took her pebbled nipples into his mouth. Ivy's back arched. She moaned. Then he removed her leggings and kissed from her ankles to her panties. Running his finger along her moist center, he slipped the material aside and circled her slickness. Ivy moaned again. Jordan slid her panties down her legs and tossed them. Ivy lay naked, giggling at his touch and enjoying how the coolness of the room licked against the heat emanating from her hot skin.

Ivy turned him over. Now she was on top. Returning the favor, she pulled Jordan's sweater over his head. Kissed his pecs. She slid her tongue down his torso over the ripples of his six-pack. His breathing quickened. Next, she loosened his belt. Tossed it aside. Ivy opened his jeans, shimmying them down the sides of his legs, then pulled them off and let them drop to the floor. She stood and looked at Jordan. Chest heaving and erection straining against his gray boxer briefs. Her eyes widened a bit at his girth. She pulled on the front of his underwear, releasing him and watching it spring to attention. A groan rose in her throat. She liked what she saw.

Jordan sat up. He reached for Ivy. Using his index finger, he outlined her body from the lips to her pelvic center and then slid his finger between her wet folds. He found her swollen bud and massaged it. Ivy's legs grew week and wobbled. Jordan stood, lifted her and gently placed her back on the bed. He showed adoration for every inch of her body, kissing, caressing, gently massaging, until Ivy felt like she would combust into a million fiery pieces.

"You're so beautiful," he rasped in her ear.

"Please," she pleaded with him breathlessly.

"Anything for you."

Jordan seemed to disappear for a quick moment. When he returned, he crawled over her, kissed her one more time and then carefully penetrated her with just the sheathed tip. Ivy's breath caught. A delicious pain shot through her and then a ravenous hunger set in. She wanted all of him inside of her. Slick with the moisture of her own juices, Jordan entered easily. He was a snug and perfect fit. His rhythm enticed her. She matched him beat by delectable beat. They rode that rhythm to a thunderous and urgent tempo.

Ivy felt herself getting ready to explode. Jordan's thrusts became more urgent. Fastening her eyes shut, she held on so they could ride their climactic wave together. His moans turned to grunts and Ivy stifled a scream. Then it happened. The dam broke. A guttural groan rose in Jordan's throat. He panted out frantic thrusts until his back arched hard. He lost his composure completely. Ivy's back arched too as her orgasm rippled through her. Together they cried out. Ivy reached a sensual height she couldn't remember reaching before. Spent, they both laid on their backs trying to catch their breaths.

Once her breathing returned to normal, Ivy felt a peace she hadn't felt in long time. With a smile on her face, she allowed herself to drift off to sleep.

That sleep was broken by the morning sun glaring through her hotel room window. Ivy blinked a few times. As the haze dissipated, she realized she was still in her hotel room. Beside her was Jordan's beautifully sculpted and naked body. His chest rose and fell steadily in sync with his light snore. It wasn't a dream. Ivy looked at the clock on the nightstand beside her bed. It was after eleven in the morning. She hadn't slept more than a full eight hours in months. It was the most peaceful sleep she'd ever remembered. Ivy chuckled, pulled the sheet over her and laid back down. It had been a good night. Careful not to wake Jordan, Ivy murmured in a low voice, "This was all that I needed."

Eighteen

Jordan woke up alone in Ivy's hotel bed. He picked up his phone and shot off a text to Anderson, who had been looking for him. Jordan was taking the day off.

He heard the faint sounds of hip-hop music and the shower running. In his full naked glory, Jordan stretched, got up from of the bed and headed to the bathroom. He knocked and waited for Ivy to respond. There was nothing. He knocked louder to make sure she heard of him over the sound of water and her own rapping. Still nothing.

Jordan turned the knob, peeked inside the steamy bath and called Ivy's name over the music. She stopped singing and pulled the curtain back.

"Hey, you," she said. "There's room for two."

Jordan grinned. "Thanks for the invitation. I'd be

happy to join you. But how about I order us some breakfast before I get in? I'm starving. That way it will arrive around the time we are done getting dressed."

"Good idea." Ivy let the curtain fall back into place and started singing again.

Jordan shook his head and laughed.

Not being sure what she wanted, Jordan ordered an array of options including fruit, eggs, waffles, coffee and juice. When he returned to the bathroom, Ivy was loudly rapping a song from one of his favorite artists. Jordan joined her in the shower and sang along. Being careful not to fall, they faced each other singing the chorus and then melted into laughter as water from the shower cascaded over them.

"I didn't peg you for a rap lover."

"There's a lot you still don't know about me, Mr. Chambers."

"I can't wait to find out more."

For several beats, no words passed between them. They stood before each other, naked, admiring one another. Ivy pulled in her bottom lip and bit it seductively. She tilted her head sweetly. Jordan instinctively licked his lips.

"Can you help me wash my back?" Ivy's voice was low and husky. She turned, giving Jordan a full view off her soft back and round bottom.

"I'm happy to help." Jordan took the cloth from her and gently rubbed soapy circles on her back.

Ivy looked over her shoulder at him. Her smile made his core tighten. When Jordan was done with her back, he wrapped his arms around her and kissed her shoulders.

"Anything else I can help you wash?" he whispered in Ivy's ear.

Ivy turned back to him, lifted onto her toes and kissed him. She guided his hand with the soapy cloth along her neck on both sides and then down her torso.

Jordan was certain that the temperature in the bathroom shot up at least ten more degrees. For the next several moments they washed each other and kissed. Jordan's erection grew rigid. He lifted Ivy into his arms. Her firm breasts pressed against his chest. Their tongues connected, entangled into a fierce passionate battle. Ivy lifted her chin. Jordan kissed her neck and rested her back against the shower wall. He wanted to enter her, but restrained his desire since he didn't have protection. Their kisses cause more steam to rise in the room.

"I want…"

Before Ivy could finish, Jordan interrupted. "I want you too."

Ivy pushed back the shower curtain. Jordan continued to hold her in his arms while carefully stepping over the side of the tub. She pushed the bathroom door open wider with her foot as he carried her back to her room. Then Jordan gingerly laid Ivy on bed and fished his last condom from his wallet. He handed it to her. She ripped the package, and rolled the protection over his stiff erection. Lifting Ivy's legs, he carefully entered, talking his time and relishing the snug, moist fit. Jordan hissed. The feel of her was too much for him to stand.

Jordan took his time. He didn't know when they would have a chance to be together like this again. He savored her, taking her with long rhythmic strokes.

Unlike the night before, they took things slow. Jordan felt like he would soon lose control. He pulled out. Ivy pleaded for him to continue. Instead, he kissed her up and down her legs. He entered her again. His strokes were steady and long. Again, he felt himself slipping away. Jordan didn't want this to end. Pulling out, he took turns suckling each nipple, then he lost himself inside her again. After a few strokes, his eyes started to roll back in his head.

Jordan removed himself from Ivy one last time. She beat the sheet with her fist. Jordan buried his face between her legs, flicked, then suckled her swollen bud. Ivy gasped and sweet moans rumbled in her throat. The sounds of her pleasure made Jordan work harder to please her. Ivy panted, bellowed a luscious and guttural melody. She grabbed a pillow and squeezed it against her chest. Jordan continued to lick until she trembled, moved back into position and entered while her orgasm claimed her body in waves.

Ivy tossed the pillow, dug her fingers into Jordan's back and pulled him to her with each thrust. A guttural moan rose from her throat, which made Jordan lose complete control. He quickened his pace from steady intentional strokes to wild bucking. Together, they convulsed over and over again. His face contorted as euphoric pleasure rippled through him like violent waves crashing against the shore. He groaned one last time before collapsing over Ivy, feeling her chest heave up and down. She wrapped her arms around him. They stayed that way for several blissful moments.

There was a knock on the door. He lifted himself high

enough to look at her. The sated smile on her face let him know that she enjoyed herself as much as he did.

"Coming!" Ivy yelled. Both of them laughed.

Their room service had arrived and the timing couldn't have been better.

"I'll get it." Jordan jumped out of bed, quickly cleaned himself with a towel and slipped into his jeans.

Grabbing his wallet, he jogged to the door and welcomed their breakfast spread. Giving the gentleman who delivered the food a healthy tip, he closed the door behind him and pushed the serving tray into the bedroom. Jordan removed his jeans and climbed back into the bed beside Ivy. She had given him so much satisfaction he was barely hungry. But that didn't stop them from feeding each other the entire hearty breakfast, bite by delicious bite between kisses.

Once they finished eating, Jordan pulled back the covers to get out of bed.

"Leaving so soon," Ivy said and pouted.

Jordan picked up his briefs and jeans. He leaned over and kissed her lips.

"You're supposed to be resting. As long as I'm around you won't get much rest."

"You've got a point." She placed her hands on the top of her head. "To be honest, I haven't felt more relaxed in months. I believe I have you to thank for that."

"You're welcome," Jordan said, grabbing his shirt.

Ivy got out of the bed and wrapped the sheet around her naked body. She walked to Jordan and placed her hand on his chest. She looked up into his eyes. "I've enjoyed your company."

He slid his arms around her waist. "I wish I didn't have to go, but you need rest." He kissed her nose.

"You're right. With you here, we haven't rested at all."

"When do you leave?" Jordan asked.

"Tomorrow. I'm heading back home for a few days. My publisher pushed some of my tour dates back so I can recuperate a little longer."

He wished she didn't have to go.

"Get some rest today and tonight. I have a few errands to run. I can come pick you up tomorrow and take you to the airport."

"That would be nice," Ivy said. She tilted her head pensively. "I think I'll book some spa treatments."

Jordan nodded. "Good idea." They kissed again. He never tired of kissing Ivy. "I have some business in New York over the next few weeks. I hope I can see you while I'm there."

"Okay. Let's work it out."

Still wrapped in her sheet, Ivy followed Jordan to the shower. They continued chatting while he dressed. At the door, they kissed one more time. They held one another like they didn't want to ever let go. Finally releasing Ivy, Jordan backed out. He winked before turning and strolling down the hallway, feeling lighter than he had in months.

Jordan had agreed to her condition about no commitments, but after spending this past day and a half with Jordan, he needed to find a way to work around that rule.

Nineteen

Ivy didn't know if it was the time she'd spent with Jordan in Los Angeles, or the days she spent at home just resting, but she felt better than she had in months. She wasn't being ushered from one place to the other, signing books, getting made up so she could look perfect as she smiled for the cameras or rushing through the airport. And she'd hardly looked at her social media profiles, which was something she usually monitored daily. She was free and that freedom felt amazing. But sadly, that didn't last long. She was now back to the grind.

Her family still didn't know about her brief visit to the hospital. If anyone asked them, she was on tour, visiting one city after the other. She'd definitely tell them eventually. The timing had to be right. However, she did miss speaking to her family. Especially Zoe. She couldn't believe she still hadn't told her anything. But Ivy couldn't risk it. Her sister-in-law had also warned her about her demanding schedule. But Ivy was sure she had this covered. She just needed a little break. Now she understood why Kendall and Tyler took long vacations where they went off the grid. But as long as she still worked for Blackwell, she couldn't get away with that. Her dad wouldn't have it.

She got ready for a team meeting over video conference. Several days a week, she'd work remotely despite being on tour. Ivy didn't want to be totally out of the loop or have a ton of worked piled up and waiting for her when she returned. She ran the women's division, so fortunately she had control over the meeting schedule unless the meeting was being planned by the company's other executives. They took her schedule into consideration.

"Hey, everybody!" Ivy waved into the camera as faces were popping up on the screen.

"Hey, Ivy," her assistant, Jess, said. "What time is it, and where are you today?"

"It's like that show *Where in the World Is Carmen* somebody. What's her name?" Zoe said.

"Sandiego," Ivy said.

"You're in San Diego?" Jess asked with a scrunched face. She helped manage some parts of Ivy's schedule, but the team at the publishing house dominated her scheduling during the tour.

"No! The girl's last name in the show is Sandiego. *Where in the World Is Carmen Sandiego?*" Zoe said.

Everyone laughed. "Gotcha!" Jess said.

"I'm in San Francisco today and will be in Seattle

tomorrow evening. I'll see you back there on Monday. I'll be home for a few days before heading out again," Ivy said.

"That's great because Dale wants to meet again. Can I put her on the schedule for next week?"

Yes! Ivy pumped her fist. She hadn't heard anything from Dale and all the waiting was making her anxious. "Hold on." She flipped through the calendar on her phone. "I'm available Wednesday or Thursday morning. Zoe, does that work for you?" Zoe checked her schedule and agreed.

"Perfect!"

Bill, Ethan and the rest of the executive team popped up on the screen.

"Looks like everyone is here," Zoe said.

"Let's get this meeting started," Bill said.

The next half hour was filled with reports on how well each region performed. The continued success with acquiring more women clients despite Dale's potential loss of business was gratifying.

"The more your face is out there, the more women we get, Ivy. Great job," Ivy's brother Ethan said. Several others joined in congratulating her.

"Thanks, Ethan. It's really empowering." Ivy was grateful for her brother's praise, but she could tell her father wasn't impressed by the stoic look on his face. He was the only one that didn't compliment her on what her presence brought to Blackwell.

Bill was old-fashioned. Despite the fact that business was thriving, he wanted Ivy to be in the office way more than she was capable of showing up. Yet her work got done. Work that she was super proud of. Work that filled that part of her that desired to make a contribution to the world that was all her own.

Another half hour passed with a few more reports and plans for the upcoming quarter. They'd had one hundred percent of Ivy's attention during the first half of the meeting, but the second half—not so much.

In the middle of the meeting, Jordan sent her a text reminding her that he'd be in New York next week and if she was in town he'd love to see her. After that, she couldn't keep her mind from conjuring up steamy thoughts about him. They'd spoken every day since she left Los Angeles, and each time she heard his voice or saw his name on her phone, he dominated her focus for a while. She was still on the fence about pursuing this "thing" with Jordan, though she could never deny that she both liked and appreciated him a lot.

Their chemistry had all the right ingredients. They enjoyed each other's company. Their conversation was stimulating and could easily flow from one subject to another. Whether they were together or on the phone, they could talk for hours. They loved the same music and some of the same favorite artists. It seemed he understood her ambition, which was a different experience for her. Ivy certainly wanted to explore more about Jordan. He seemed perfect, which was scary.

And in bed? Whew! Jordan was *amazing*. He'd make love to her body and soul. He was a patient lover— something she didn't realize she loved. She could easily see herself becoming addicted to Jordan but that wouldn't be good. Would it?

What was going to happen once they started filming the show? Hollywood was funny place. She already started to get more attention from social media. Her following increased significantly after the incident with Kenya at the awards show. They spiked again once the book was released and now Ivy spent more time monitoring her social media. More brands wanted to work with her. However, not all of the attention she received on social media was good. Kenya had been blocked so she didn't see much from her, but there was other "haters" out there. Trolls were coming at her left and right. Her team tried to delete their negative comments before they stirred any trouble. They didn't like Ivy seeing those comments because she hadn't learned how to ignore them yet. That was just something influencers had to deal with. Still, Ivy couldn't understand why people were so mean.

Jordan texted her again. This time, he mentioned some special place he'd like to take her. Ivy waited until the meeting ended. Instead of texting him back, she called just to hear his voice.

"Hey!" Jordan's deep voice flowed through the phone making her wish he wasn't over three hundred miles away. "How are you feeling?"

Ivy felt her lips ease into a smile. It happened every time she heard his voice. "Great. Thanks for asking."

"Did you get my text?"

"I did. What's this special place you're talking about?"

"Nope! No details for you. That's a secret. Just let me know when you're available so I can make the arrangements. One night with you will do."

"Hmm. Top secret. And just one night, huh? Sounds like the makings of a steamy romance novel."

"Ha! I hope you enjoy it just the same."

"I have a feeling I will. Let me check my calendar." Ivy reviewed her availability and let Jordan know that Friday would work best. As a single hardworking woman with a ridiculously busy schedule, Friday nights tended to be uneventful unless she was traveling. She hardly had time to hang with the girls.

"This is perfect. I'll be in on Wednesday evening," Jordan said.

"Let me know what time. Maybe I can pick you up at the airport."

"I'll text the times. If not, I have a service that I use."

"Cool. Gotta run but I look forward to seeing you next week."

Just as Ivy ended the call with Jordan, her phone rang again. It was her dad.

"Hi, Dad."

"Hi, honey." He called her *honey*, but his voice was void of any sweetness. "We need to talk."

Twenty

Jordan shut down his laptop, stuffed it in the carrying case and stood. There was no point in trying to concentrate on work any longer. He was heading to New York and the thought of being in the same city as Ivy had stolen his focus all morning. Thinking about her made him smile. Remembering their conversation and her words *fun while it lasted* made him wonder if the fun could ever run out. He'd enjoyed every minute of every conversation with Ivy since she'd left.

He looked at his watch, realizing he had just an hour to get to the airport. There was no need for luggage when he had a penthouse in New York that was just as packed as his luxury condo in LA. His laptop was his travel companion. Maybe he'd manage to get some work done in the airport lounge or on the plane.

Suddenly, Anderson burst through Jordan's office door. "Did you see the email?"

"What email?" Jordan asked.

Anderson stepped all the way in "They literally just sent it—the production schedule. They want to start filming next month. They're ready to move on this one."

"Fix My Money?" Jordan asked. They had other shows in the works but were most excited about their show with Ivy.

"We've got some details to work out. Call me when you get through airport security. I don't want this to wait until you land."

"No problem."

"In the meantime," Anderson continued, "I'll compile some of the things they asked about in the email. I'll run it by you when we talk. We've got great contestants lined up ready to go."

"This is going to be great! I'll check out the email on the way to the airport. My car should be here any minute."

The fast pace of the industry had always excited the two of them. Recently, things had changed drastically. It used to take months or longer to get a deal done on a show and get a production schedule in place. Now, with such a high demand for content and so many channels and streaming options, decisions were being made in record time. Everyone wanted to grab the most compelling content as soon as possible.

The show was being produced in Los Angeles, which meant that Jordan would see a lot more of Ivy. Being on set would require them to make sure they kept their composure and remained professional. Jordan had no problem with that.

Instead of waiting until he got to the airport, Jordan called Anderson while he was in the car. They went over details and next steps. Once Jordan got through security, he settled in the airline's lounge, ordered a glass of scotch and phoned Ivy.

"We've got something to celebrate but first, how are you feeling?" Jordan asked.

"Not bad. I managed to sleep off my jet lag after my trip to San Francisco. What are we celebrating?" Jordan could hear the excitement in Ivy's voice and was glad he was the one that could share the news with her.

"You'll get a call from your team, but I wanted to be the first to let you know that the network is ready to move forward. They sent a production schedule and would like to start shooting next month!" Jordan was expecting Ivy to laugh, shout, scream—something.

After a few moments of silence, Ivy finally said, "Wow."

"Shocked, huh?"

"Well, yes. Shocked and a bit nervous. This is so new to me. What if I mess up? What if I forget my lines? I have to clear my schedule. What—"

"Whoa! Take a breath," Jordan soothed. "And don't worry…this is a reality show. There aren't really any lines to remember. You're the expert, Ivy. You'll do what you normally do, tell people how to build wealth. It's just that your 'clients' will be rather…interesting since most of them are celebrities or celebrity adjacent. They won't be anything like your regular clientele."

Ivy snorted. "Yeah. Spoiled rich brats who go

through money like water. This *is* going to be interesting. Wow. I can't wait. I have to run. See you when you get here?"

"Yes. And thanks for offering to pick me up at the airport, but don't worry about it," he told her. "I'm arriving early to take care of some family business. But I'd love to see you after that. Think you'll be up for a late dinner?"

"Around what time?" Jordan sensed the hesitancy in Ivy's tone. He knew her schedule had been packed, and while he really wanted to see her, he didn't want to burden her knowing she still needed to rest as much as possible between tour dates, speaking engagements and work.

"Is eight too late? I'll come to you. You pick the place."

"Works for me. Maybe you can help me relax a bit more." Ivy snickered.

"Ha! I can definitely do that." Jordan laughed knowing that Ivy was talking about being intimate. They joked about how relaxed they felt after being together at her hotel previously. Whether they made love or not, being with Ivy calmed him.

Jordan's phone vibrated. It was a text letting him know his flight was boarding. Finishing off his drink, he headed to the gate. Either he was tired or his first-class seat was comfortable because Jordan didn't remember taking off. He'd woken up at the rumble caused by the airplane's wheels making contact with the runway.

Jordan's brother, Dorian, picked him up at the airport and they headed to his mother's house.

"My boys!" Charisse came running out of the house when they pulled up.

Their mom looked stunning in smart-looking navy slacks and a matching blouse with a large bow at the top. She embraced them tight as she always did.

"Come on in. Are you hungry? I have some leftovers in the fridge. I've been busy all day and didn't have time to make anything. How about a drink? You boys want a drink?"

"That would be nice," Dorian said, heading to the refrigerator and retrieving two bottles of water. He tossed one to Jordan.

Jordan twisted the cap and downed half the bottle. "Ah! I didn't realize I was that thirsty."

Charisse pulled a bottle of scotch and three glasses from the spirits cabinet and placed them on the table in the living room. She was responsible for Jordan and Dorian's appreciation of top-shelf scotch. Their mom taught them things that fathers usually taught their boys. Things like how to drive and how to drink properly, explaining to them the difference between the finer selections and the cheap stuff. She also taught them to sip casually and not gulp, which she considered classless. Their mom insisted that would only get them drunk prematurely. Jordan poured an inch of scotch in each glass and handed them out. They followed Charisse into the living room.

"Come." She patted the sofa beside her. "Sit. It will be a few minutes before Tim gets here."

"So, what did he have to say about our proposal?" Jordan asked.

Charisse smiled at him. "Looks like we're getting right down to business."

Jordan raised his glass as a response. His mom and Dorian touched glasses with his and the three of them sipped.

"Here's the deal," Charisse said and placed her glass down on the coffee table.

Jordan held his sigh in, bracing himself for what his mother was about to say. He glanced at Dorian, who was already looking his way. The way their mother started made him think they may not like the answer.

"Tim most certainly needs your help, but doesn't feel like the arrangement we proposed is in his best interest."

"What? I thought—"

"Hold on." Charisse held up her hand. "He's a prideful man. I don't have to remind you boys that your relationship with him has always been a bit...strained."

"But this is a solid business offer, Ma." Dorian said the very words that Jordan wanted to say. "Did you tell him this proposal was your idea?"

"I did." Charisse sighed. "It's just hard for him. Asking you two for help isn't easy. And I think that he just wants to make sure he has some say in how this proposal is finalized. He doesn't want to feel bulldozed just because he needs help."

"What's that supposed to mean?" Dorian snapped, looking between Jordan and his mother.

Door locks clicked. Jordan, Dorian and Charisse's focus shifted to Tim stepping in. He was a tall, strapping man whose only hint of his years was a neatly shaven salt-and-pepper beard. Tension rose in the room immediately.

"Hello, honey." Tim's long strides swept across the floor, taking him to Charisse's side quickly. He kissed her lips.

"Hello, sweetie," she said, touching his cheek and wiping her lipstick from his lips.

"Jordan. Dorian." Tim nodded at both of them. They nodded back. The greeting was devoid of any warmth.

Jordan noticed Tim's eyes dart between their drinks on the table.

"Give me a moment and I'll join you."

Jordan sat back in his chair and hoped this interaction would be painless.

Tim poured his own drink and joined them in the living room, sitting next to his wife. Charisse took his free hand in hers.

"I'll assume you've been chatting about this arrangement."

"Yes. It appears you have an issue with the proposal?" Jordan asked. He had no time for small talk.

"It's a good deal," Dorian added.

"I didn't say it wasn't." Tim huffed. "But it's my company and I'm not signing anything without having my input and interest fully represented."

"What?" Dorian said. "Mom!"

"You guys made this arrangement with her. Not me. This company supports her but it's not hers."

Both boys looked at their mom.

"So, what do you propose?" Jordan asked, feeling himself becoming irritated. "What specific aspects of the contract do you have a problem with?"

"All of it!" Tim yelled.

"Timothy," Charisse admonished.

Jordan knew where this was going. Tim felt emasculated because he had nothing to do with the terms. While he understood that, they had no time to engage in pissing matches with this man while his company quickly went under.

"I don't want you as partners. I just need a loan. I'll pay it back. I've been in business for over twenty-five years." Tim stabbed the air with his index finger as he spoke. "I know what I'm doing, and I'm not selling off my stakes in a business I built because of one rough spot. I've been in rough spots before and never folded." Tim stood and paced. "I know you guys don't think that well of me, but despite that, I took good care of you boys and gave your mother the best life I could possibly provide for her. But no matter what I did, it was never good enough for you guys. I asked for help. I don't need your pity and I won't be taken advantage of. And I won't let you stand by and take my business from me."

"Timothy!" Charisse cried. "No one is trying to take advantage of you!"

"Or take your business," Jordan said. "This was supposed to help."

"Help who?" Tim shouted. He then proceeded to rant on about their intentions, ending with, "Just forget about it. I don't want any help from either of you." He glared at Jordan and then Dorian.

Jordan couldn't believe what was he was hearing. Tim had said things that angered him but they hurt as well. What made him believe that Dorian and Jordan would take advantage of him or try to take his business? Despite not getting along, they never acted without integrity.

Dorian stood and popped his collar. "I'm out of here." He walked over to Charisse. "Ma, I love you, but I've got to go." He hugged Charisse and kissed her cheek.

Their mom stood now too. Her shoulders slumped. "Wait. We have to talk this out." She turned to Timothy. "Listen, honey, that's not what we intended here. This is to help and protect all of our interests."

"Not mine!" he barked.

Jordan hugged his mother. He was on the same page as Dorian. "Love you, Mom." He kissed her cheek too. "But there doesn't look like there's much to talk about."

"I don't need to bow to your boys. I'll get through this myself."

"Timothy!"

Jordan heard the man continue to protest as he and his brother exited. Leaving was the best thing for them to do. Things would have gotten ugly. Jordan was sure Dorian wouldn't have had a problem issuing Tim a loan, but his words cut, accusing them of trying to take advantage of him, steal his business. Never. Jordan would rather not deal with Tim at all than to be accused of being underhanded.

In spite of his hurt and anger, Jordan was torn. Tim definitely needed their help but was too stubborn to take it. And their mom was caught in the middle.

Outside, Dorian stalked from the front of the car to the back with his hands on his hips. "Can you believe the nerve of this man?"

Jordan massaged his throbbing temples. "No. I can't."

"I need another drink. Want to join me?" Dorian said once he finally got in the car and slammed the door.

"Sure," Jordan agreed. He huffed. Somehow, he

knew he would have to be the one to fix this situation. Another drink would help but being with Ivy would be even better. Nothing would take the edge off like time alone with her.

Twenty-One

"Oh, no!" Ivy yelled. She threw back the comforter, moved Jordan's arm from around her waist and jumped out of bed. "I can't be late."

Ivy felt Jordan's eyes on her bare bottom as she ran to the master bathroom. She turned on the shower and held her hand under the flow of water for a few moments. That was a habit of hers. After a quick shower, she covered herself in a towel and rummaged through her walk-in closet to find something that didn't require ironing. Normally, Ivy would take out her clothes the night before, but once Jordan got to her home, she'd forgotten all about that.

Ivy had been excited to see Jordan, but when he arrived in a sullen mood, she turned her focus on putting a smile on his face. She'd been stressed about work and he'd been stressed about the situation with his parents. Their lovemaking was slow and deep as if they were filling all the gaps in each other's lives. They soothed one another's woes and fell asleep wrapped in each other's arms. Between the news that Jordan shared about her new television show and the way he held her, Ivy's stress all but melted away.

Until now.

Ivy needed to get to work on time today. She had a meeting with her dad and was due to connect with Dale. She grabbed a light sweater dress, undergarments and boots and headed back to the bedroom. Jordan had made his way into her shower. Ivy almost wished she could take the day and spend it in his arms. However, both of them had full schedules. She'd get to spend more quality time with him during the evening Jordan had planned for them. He still wouldn't tell her anything about it.

Ivy peeked into the bathroom. "Morning! I'm heading down. Want coffee to go?"

"Sure! Thanks," Jordan said over the water. "I have a car coming. He can drop you off and take me to my meeting."

Ivy looked at her watch. "Really? That would be great!" This ride into the city was going to save her time. She should get to work on time so she could face her father.

An hour later, Ivy was kissing Jordan goodbye. She jumped out of the car in front of Blackwell's headquarters. Inside she made it to her office without running into her dad. Ivy sat, turned to the window and took in the view of the city's skyline. With a deep breath in and a long breath out, she closed her eyes and calmed herself. She dreaded this meeting with her dad. He had questions for her. She had answers for some of them, but they weren't the ones he was looking for. She couldn't understand why he couldn't just be proud of her.

When her phone buzzed, she didn't even bother to look at her text messages. She stood, tugged on the front of her suit jacket and straightened her back. It was time to face Bill.

Ivy passed Zoe's office. She could hear her on the phone. She waved. Then she passed Ethan's office. Peeking in, she saw that he was on the phone as well. She greeted him with a nod and a smile, then stepped out and closed his door. Ivy sighed. She was procrastinating. Squaring her shoulders, she headed straight for Bill's office.

The door was ajar. Ivy lifted her hand to knock but before her knuckles connected with the wood, Bill said, "Come on in."

"Hey… Dad." Ivy wrung her hands. Her anxiety flowed from her stomach to the extremities. Sinking down into the leather tufted seat in front of his desk, she tapped her foot and toyed with her freshly manicured nails.

It took several moments for Bill to glance up from his laptop. When he did, he pulled off his glasses and held them loosely. He looked at her and sat back in his massive leather chair. "Good morning, my daughter."

Outside of work, Bill often called her "baby girl." He'd called her daughter when he wanted to make a statement.

"Father." She was being as formal as he was.

"Let's start with the state of the deal with Dale," Bill said, placing his glasses down and folding his hands.

"I'm meeting with her today. We're a step closer to closing the deal. She loves the fact that we've been getting so much exposure regarding our women's initiatives, but she really wanted to make sure her investments were getting the best attention." She swallowed. "I assured her that they would be and gave her some insight into how our executive team is vital in making sure the investment strategies attempt to get us the best possible returns."

"Let's cut to the chase here, Ivy," Bill said, sitting back in his chair. "The bottom line is that this new initiative has been quite successful. You deserve full credit for that. But this isn't going to be successful without you. You asked for this position. I gave it you. You've proved yourself, but it can't continue to grow if you're not focused or you're not here. The exposure is good, but people want to know that you're part of the deal when they transfer their assets over to Blackwell. And lately, you just haven't been around."

Ivy sighed. "Dad." Bill tilted his head. He was listening. But all she could think about was how he'd respond to the fact that she got this show and it would require her to be in Los Angeles to shoot for several weeks. "Zoe is just as capable as me. She's my partner on this initiative."

"But Zoe's public image is not tied to Blackwell the way yours is. You're selling these people something that when they come to Blackwell they're not seeing. Do you know a client reached out because she was unable to connect with you for days while you were on tour? You're usually much more responsive. What happened?" Bill shook his head. "I'm excited for you and your book, but, Ivy, this is affecting business."

Ivy felt deflated. Her posture matched how she felt on the inside. There was so much she wanted to say to her father. Things like, what about what *she* wanted? That customer had been looking for her while she was in the hospital. She couldn't tell Bill about that yet. It would prove his point that things were falling through the cracks because she had too much on her plate.

"My book tour will be over soon and my schedule won't be as busy," she said.

"Honey. If it's not the tour, it's a conference, a speaking engagement or something else."

Ivy thought about the show when he said that. She had to be in LA in thirty days. She wanted to tell him, but couldn't bring herself do it just yet.

"I just need a little more time." Ivy didn't want to disappoint him. "The tour will be done in two more weeks. I'm sure you realize the conferences and speaking engagements will continue but that's how we've gotten so many of our new women clients. Those engagements have been great for business." She was proud of what she'd started at Blackwell. Bill was right, she'd asked for this. But she also didn't want to disappoint herself.

Despite being exhausted, she deserved to enjoy all the amazing opportunities heading her way. It was new, different and exciting. Being the Money Maven pulled her entirely out of her comfort zone in the most dynamic ways. It was a life she created outside of the Blackwell name. The publisher, Jordan, the networks and her audience were less concerned about her being a Blackwell.

They loved the profile she'd created with the help of her branding and social media team. Ivy never imagined she'd have her own show. How could she say no to that?

Ivy swallowed a lump in her throat. She remembered Kendall and Tyson's advice when they suggested she may have to quit Blackwell. It was looking more and more like having her position at Blackwell and her life as the Money Maven was becoming impossible to maintain simultaneously.

"I need to see some significant changes…" she heard Bill say. Ivy had gotten lost in her thoughts. "After this whole—" Bill waved his hand dismissively "—*book tour* thing is over, I need you to focus on your department. Your objectives. I built this company for my children. First Lincoln left. Then Carter. Looks like you're on your way out too. And for what? Your mother and I have broken our backs to give you everything. What more do you need?" And there it was, the "after all we've done for you" speech.

It was true. In the past few years, all but Ethan had walked away from Blackwell to pursue other opportunities. Each of them seemed to be walking away from the legacy Bill and Lydia worked so hard to create for them. Again, guilt and anger swirled in her chest, feeling like a bad case of heartburn. Ivy swallowed. She understood Bill's desire to create a legacy. It was notable. But had he even once asked her what she wanted?

Twenty-Two

Jordan kissed Ivy's lips. He took his forefinger and gently touched the tip of her nose, where the light of the morning sun had settled. He wanted to wake up next to her every day. Ivy giggled under his touch.

"Today's your big day. How do you feel?" he asked, facing her as he lay on his side. Crisp white sheets covered their naked bodies.

"I can't even put my feelings into words," Ivy said. "I still can't believe I have my own television show. Oh, my goodness!" She laid on her back, squeezed her eyes shut and squealed. "I have a television show!"

Jordan chuckled, happy about his role in making her smile. At one point he thought this deal was never going to happen. Their production schedule was delayed by almost six additional weeks. Even the season had changed. Ivy was glad to be in Los Angeles because Old Man Winter had a heck of a grip on New York. She hadn't bothered to book a hotel for her stay in LA. Jordan's condo had become their regular hangout. The only benefit to the frustrating delays was the fact that Jordan and Ivy got to spend so much time together before the show started shooting.

"We need to get dressed so we can get down to the studio. We've got a long day ahead of us," Ivy said, turning back toward Jordan.

"Yeah. Right after this." He wrapped his arms around Ivy and pulled her on top of him. "Do you see what you do to me?"

Ivy showered his face with kisses. Tenderness spread through Jordan. Being with Ivy, feeling her touch, seeing her smile, being the subject of her undivided attention—all of these things made his chest warm on the inside. He couldn't ever remember a woman's attention making him feel this way.

Jordan drew Ivy even closer to him. Skin to skin, they stared deep into each other's eyes. There was something about this woman. Something that Jordan couldn't put into words. Her presence in his life over the past few months felt right in every way.

Staring up at her, he searched Ivy's eyes. He hoped she was as enamored with him as he was with her. Jordan felt his erection growing, standing at attention between them. He wanted to feel her. He wanted to be inside of her. However, he didn't want to stop admiring Ivy. He ran his finger through her hair. Kissed her nose. Then ran his thumb across her lips and claimed her mouth with his. Ivy looked back at him and blinked.

Pulling back, he watched her pretty lashes flutter and gently kissed each lid.

As he continued basking in her, Ivy reached down and wrapped her hand around his erection. Jordan's core tightened. Instinctively, his eyes closed briefly. He felt Ivy's lips on his. Their kiss was passionate. Deep. Hungry. Jordan licked a scorching trail from Ivy's lips to her navel. He spread her legs, circled his tongue along her love canal before gently nibbling on her bud. She hissed. Jordan smiled. Ivy's excitement excited him. He couldn't get enough of her.

Jordan continued nibbling until Ivy's moans grew louder and louder, compelling Jordan to please her more. He wrapped his hand around her hips and worked her bud until she beat the sheets with her fists and howled. Lifting himself, he entered her slickness. All the while, Ivy gasped and groped at Jordan. His sweat-covered body wouldn't allow her to get a good grip.

Jordan drove himself inside of Ivy, burying his shaft deep within her. Her walls tightened around him, giving him pleasure so profound he could feel himself slipping into euphoria.

"Ivy!" Her name slipped from his lips in a whisper.

"Jordan." She said his name and the sound was so wondrous to his ears that his heart clenched.

Together they found a glorious rhythm and rode each other until Jordan's skin prickled with sweet, sweltering heat and the pain of too much pleasure.

"Ivy. Ivy." He called her name with each downstroke. His body bucked, making his rhythm staccato. "Ivy," Jordan grunted.

"Jordan!" Ivy was breathless. She dug her fingernails into his backside, pushing him deeper inside of her. "Oh, Jordan!"

"Ivy." Jordan pumped faster. He could feel the quickened pace of his heart. Another second inside of her and he was going to blow. "Ivy... I..." Jordan's eyes popped open. He looked down at her moving under him and blinked. Her eyes were closed and the look of pure pleasure was plastered across her face. She was caught up in the moment. Blissfully unaware of what almost came out of his mouth. Jordan tried not to lose his rhythm. Closing his eyes, he found a new tempo and hung on to it until Ivy cried out and shuddered. His peak ripped through him with the fire and force of a shooting star. Jordan groaned. His abdomen tightened. His strokes became short, urgent and fast until the dam broke inside of him. Jordan removed himself and felt the life flow from him in back-shattering waves. Together their bodies went limp.

With eyes closed, Ivy snuggled against his damp chest. She snaked her arms around his torso and squeezed him to her. Jordan's eyes were fixed on the sunlight glowing orange outside the window. They had to get going but he didn't want to move. His heart was still pumping rapidly. Not because he'd just had the best sex of his life, but because he'd almost shouted that he loved Ivy in the middle of it.

Jordan didn't move. He just let Ivy stay there in his arms, sated, as his mind analyzed what had just happened. He replayed all that had transpired between the evening he'd first seen Ivy at the wrap event right up to her being in his arms tonight.

Over the last few weeks, they had spent every possible moment together. He visited New York and she visited Los Angeles often. They commuted to each other as if they were a mere subway ride away. Jordan would also meet her in other cities when she traveled.

They were doing more than having fun. Jordan and Ivy were having the time of their lives. He made note of all the things that brought her joy and made a sport of spoiling Ivy. He hadn't met her family, but from their long conversations and all of the pillow talk, he felt like he already knew them. They hadn't actually labeled their commitment, but Jordan certainly hadn't thought of entertaining any other women. Despite a lack of definition, what they shared was special to Jordan. They hadn't set out to keep their dating a secret, but very few people knew about them.

Jordan had only just mentioned Ivy to Dorian. He couldn't keep anything from Anderson, so he hadn't tried, knowing he could trust him implicitly. Jordan knew that Ivy's sister-in-law Zoe knew about them. But she was Ivy's keeper of secrets. Both Jordan and Ivy preferred to keep their love lives low-key for two reasons. First, because they valued their privacy, and second, because they wanted to keep their work interactions professional.

They were usually successful in keeping their connection under wraps but sometimes the intense chemistry between them would ooze into the atmosphere. They'd laugh about it later over dinner or in bed.

"Jordan," Ivy called his name, bringing him back to the present. Her sultry voice made him want to make love to her again but they were running out of time.

He kissed her forehead. "Yeah?"

"We have to go," she said.

"I know."

Instead of getting out of the bed, Ivy straddled him, wrapped her palm around his limpness and massaged him back to life. It didn't take long at all. She guided him inside of her and rode him until a cacophony of groans and moans created a sultry chorus.

Finally, they dressed and headed to the studio. Jordan's thoughts keep slipping back to what he'd almost said in the sizzling heat of the moment. Had he meant what he was about to say or was it a case of temporary incredible sexual insanity?

Twenty-Three

Ivy went to the studio by car service. Jordan drove. It was her idea. Neither wanted to leave the bed they'd come to share regularly. Ivy wasn't necessarily hiding the fact that she was dating Jordan; she was simply keeping her business to herself. Jordan was her delicious little secret. More importantly, they wanted to keep things professional for the sake of the show. Being the Money Maven was her public profile, but Ivy Blackwell appreciated her privacy. Which was becoming more and more difficult to manage.

She had been wondering where things were going with them for a while now but didn't want to be the one to bring it up. They could revisit that after shooting the show. Jordan had become like a balm. Being with him soothed Ivy. Just hearing his voice helped to ease real pressures of her busy life whether he was in person or over the phone. He'd become a confidant, a voice of reason and the person she bounced ideas off of.

Jordan encouraged her to fly Dale Billington out to the studio to watch the filming of the show. He helped her convince Dale that all the opportunities that Ivy enjoyed helped to raise the profile for Ivy, Blackwell and her clients, bringing Dale another step closer to signing with them. Jordan was brilliant when it came to working with picky clientele.

Ivy's car pulled up to the studio. She opened her window to take it all in. The driver rolled through the studio arriving at a trailer with Ivy's name on it. Giggles bubbled out of her. She couldn't contain herself!

Exiting the car, Ivy took in the trailer, covered her mouth and shook her head. Both her names were on the trailer, Ivy Blackwell and the Money Maven. A young woman with a clipboard walked up to her.

"Morning, Money Maven." She held out her small hand. Her petite stature didn't match her booming voice. Ivy like her immediately.

"Good morning…" Ivy paused.

"Hailey," the woman said and they shook hands.

"Good morning, Hailey."

"Let's get you settled in and ready to start."

Ivy smiled. She was never at a loss for words, but didn't know what else to say. She followed Hailey to her trailer so she could put her things down and then they toured the set. More people arrived, including Jordan and Anderson. Ivy was carried off to wardrobe to pick out a few outfits and meet some of the celebs she would be working with to fix their finances. After hours of prep, they were finally ready to shoot a few scenes.

Ivy's excitement managed to help keep her mind off Jordan. Yet, several times, she'd catch a glimpse of him in action. Ivy was impressed at how he navigated the set, gave orders or interacted with the crew. When she thought no one was looking, she'd allow herself a moment to study his handsome face, broad shoulders and taut chest. His smile made her swoon even from a distance. What Ivy hadn't expected was the twinge of jealousy that squiggled through her when she realized that she wasn't the only woman on the set eyeing him.

That unexpected envy had thrown her when the crew was trying to capture a few video clips of her around the set that were going be used in the show's opening. She was supposed to be posing for videos and photos but her eyes kept wandering toward Jordan on the other side of the studio. He was speaking to a woman who kept rubbing this arm.

Ivy shook it off but watching the woman dote on him put a damper on her excitement. At one point the director, Carly, followed Ivy's line of sight to Jordan all the way on the other side of the set. She looked away, hoping the woman didn't realize she had been watching Jordan. During a break, she grabbed a granola bar, and her stomach lurched when the director came over to examine the snacks at the food table.

"Doing okay?" Carly asked.

"Me?" Ivy asked.

"Yes. First day going okay?"

"Yes. This is very thrilling."

"Good," Carly said and fell silent for a moment while she studied Ivy. "Just be careful."

"Careful of what?"

"You're not the only woman around here with their eyes on Jordan Chambers. Every eligible chick wants a piece of him. He doesn't exactly wear himself thin like most of the other producers out here, which is why he's in demand. Competition is stiff around here." Carly chuckled. "Vicious and relentless too," she said before walking off.

Ivy wanted to ask Carly what she meant by that but bit her tongue. That would let the director know she was interested in Jordan, and what they had was their secret. However, Carly's words did fire off a bunch more questions in Ivy's mind. They also planted some seeds of worry and doubt. How many women on the set were after Jordan? Had anyone else noticed how she'd studied him? Would they make things difficult on the set?

By the time the day ended, Ivy convinced herself that dating Jordan while the show was in production wasn't a good idea. She found herself wondering about who he was likely to spend time with while she was back in New York.

Ivy groaned aloud as she paced her trailer during another break. Why was she even worried about women crushing on Jordan? What did she care about who he was spending his time with when she was in New York? Ivy had never been the jealous type. And she and Jordan has intentionally avoided labeling what they had together. None of this stuff should have mattered to Ivy. Yet all of it did.

Ivy popped open one of the sparkling waters stored

in her refrigerator. Sat down and pulled out her cell phone. She hadn't noticed her parents' and brothers' messages in their family chat. They were asking about the first day of shooting. Her father still wasn't 100 percent on board, but her brothers had convinced him that good things would come from this. The delays to the start of the shooting schedule did give Ivy the time she needed to prepare him for the fact that she would need a six-week leave to be in LA to film the show. Only Zoe knew that she was staying with Jordan instead of renting a place of her own. It was his idea. They'd agreed that she could check into the hotel whenever she felt like she needed space.

Ivy sent them a few pictures of the set that she'd taken throughout the day. She uploaded a fun selfie of her pointing to her name on the side of the trailer to her social media profiles.

There were two short hard knocks on Ivy's door. She looked at the time on her cell to make sure she hadn't overstayed her break time.

"Coming!" she said, assuming it was one of the production assistants coming to get her.

Ivy opened the door to find Jordan standing on the other side.

"Hey. Come on in." Ivy nervously scanned the area outside of her trailer. Had someone seen him come inside? Did it matter?

Jordan stepped in and looked around. Ivy glanced around one more time before closing the door behind him.

"You happy with the trailer? I told them to take good care of you," he murmured, stepping closer to her.

Ivy turned, walked over to grab her bottle of sparkling water and took a sip. "It's great. Why did you tell them to do that?"

"We do that for all of our major talent."

"Oh...okay. Thanks. It's fine," Ivy said.

Jordan narrowed his eyes at her. "Are you okay?"

"Yeah. I'm fine."

He tilted his head and studied her for a moment. "You sure?"

Ivy chuckled and waved away his concern. "I'm sure."

"Still excited?"

"Absolutely!"

Jordan closed the space between them and slid his arms around her waist. "We will celebrate your first full day when we get home."

Home. Jordan had said the word as if his home was also her home. Everything that Carly said about other women pursuing Jordan flooded Ivy's mind. Was she doing the right thing?

Before she could protest, Jordan put his lips on hers. She closed her eyes and melted in his embrace.

Ivy wiped her lipstick from Jordan's lips when they finished kissing. "Maybe we shouldn't be doing this here."

"Who's going to know?" Jordan asked, shrugging.

"I'm just saying." Ivy pulled away. "We said we would keep it professional on set."

Jordan held his hand up. "You're right. I just wanted to check on you. I have to run. Meet you back at my house later?"

"Sure."

Jordan kissed her before leaving her trailer. His kiss,

as passionate as all the others, seemed to lift her off her feet. The second he left, the reality of how close they were cutting things came crashing down on her again. What was she doing?

She sat down and gathered her emotions. They were all over the place. If they needed her on the set, they'd send a production assistant to get her. She checked in with Dale, who was supposed to arrive that day. The next day, she would come to visit the set like Jordan suggested.

Ivy's phone buzzed indicating that she had another text message. It was an image and link from Zoe with a text that said, Have you seen this?

What came up shocked Ivy. The link took her to a gossip site's media profile displaying several pictures of her and Jordan at different times over the past week. The caption said, "Is the Money Maven 'fixing' more than just celebrity's finances while in LA?"

Ivy covered her mouth. Where had this come from?

Twenty-Four

Jordan sat with his head in his hands. The day couldn't have started better. He'd woken up beside Ivy, relished her excitement of the first day of her show and made sweet love to her. What the heck happened to get them to where they were now?

He watched Ivy stuff her belongings in her suitcase and frantically explain why she had to go.

"This doesn't make sense to me, Ivy." He was exasperated.

"I don't know how else to say this, Jordan. This—" she looked around and then pointed to him and then her "—wasn't a good idea. We just got carried away. I mean, it was fun while it lasted but this is proof that it was a bad idea!" Ivy held up her phone displaying the social media post speculating about their involvement.

"My family has seen this, and now they're concerned about some kind of viral scandal blowing up and making us look bad." Ivy flopped down on the chaise across from Jordan's massive king-size bed. Her head hung low and she closed her eyes.

"This is all part of being a public figure. You can't let this kind of stuff affect you!"

"Well, I haven't learned how to do that yet. It's bothering the heck out of me. I don't want to be the subject of anybody's attention-seeking headline to get some likes and clicks."

"You gave up that option when you became the Money Maven," Jordan said, and Ivy's head snapped in his direction. She looked like she would burst into tears at any moment.

"I'm sorry but it's the truth. Ugh!" Jordan stood and paced. After a few moments, he huffed and turned to Ivy. "Just let your family know that this kind of stuff is part of the process. Explain that to your parents. I'm pretty sure your brothers get it."

"You don't understand, Jordan." Ivy's shoulders slumped.

"So, what are you going to do? Stop being the Money Maven? No social media, no speaking events, no more workshops and no show?" Jordan asked. Ivy rubbed her temples. "Because that's what it's going to take for the gossip sites and internet trolls to back off. You'd have to be insignificant to them. Stop reading that crap and keep doing all the amazing things you've been doing."

Her hands flopped into her lap. "It's one thing to see this happen to others. But it's me. This doesn't feel good. Look what happened at the awards and now this.

My parents are furious, asking me all kinds of crazy questions that I can't answer. It's too much! How am I supposed to just ignore it all?"

"By continuing to be you. You love helping women. Keep doing that." Jordan pivoted like he had a great idea. "We could get in front of this, you know."

"How?"

"We put something out on our own social media," he proposed. "Let people know we're seeing each other. It's no big deal."

Ivy took a deep breath. She finally stood. "That's not going to work, Jordan. It will look like I got this opportunity because I was sleeping with you. That's the last thing I want."

Jordan grunted. "It doesn't have to be that way."

Ivy threw her hands up. "Stop. I need to go."

"Why?"

"If I'm going to be any good on set. I need to keep a clear head, and with all that's going on, it's becoming harder to do."

Jordan clenched his jaw. "You're talking about us, aren't you?" He stepped closer to her. Ivy took a step back as he approached. "What happened today?" He reached out for Ivy. She moved out of his reach. "Did I do something?" Jordan asked incredulously. He was hurt and confused.

"No." Her voice was just above a whisper. "I just… we took this too far, too soon. I…don't want this to look the wrong way." She started pacing again. "We need to put space between us at least until after we're done with filming."

"Where are you going to go?" Jordan folded his arms,

unfolded them and put his thumb and index finger on
his forehead.

"I'll stay at a hotel." She flipped her hand as if it
were no big deal.

"You don't have to do this." Frustration rose in him.
He didn't mean to sound harsh. Jordan was just having
a hard time keeping his emotions in check. This was
the woman that he almost admitted his love for less
than twenty-four hours ago. Everything was great then.
Now, things were drastically different and he couldn't
understand why. "What about our plans for tonight?
What about this weekend? Dale is coming to the set
tomorrow."

"I'm sorry, Jordan."

"This social media stuff will die down. All we—"

"I'm dealing with it the best way I know how," Ivy
interjected.

"By running away from everything? By running
away from *me*?" Jordan jabbed his chest.

"Especially you."

Jordan felt as if he'd been kicked in the chest. He
reared his head back.

"This is my profession. It's an amazing opportunity.
I can't have it tainted with some kind of crazy scandal.
I'm sorry but I have to do this."

Jordan stood, shaking his head. He wasn't a scandal.
He loved this woman. She just didn't know it. Maybe
he should have told her but that window of opportunity
had passed. Saying it now wouldn't change anything.
If Ivy wanted to go, he'd have to let her no matter how
bad he wanted her to stay. He would never be the one
to keep company that didn't want to be kept.

He lifted his hands up in defeat. Biting his lip, he fought to reel in his emotions. He turned, stepped into the walk-in closet in the en suite and came back with keys.

"Here." He handed them to Ivy, who was facing the window with her arms folded.

"What is this?"

"Keys to my company's corporate apartment. We keep it for special guests. If you have to leave here, stay there. You don't have to go to a hotel. Plus, you'll have much more privacy."

Ivy looked at the keys a moment before taking them. "What's the address?"

Jordan looked at her. After several moments ticked by, he said, "It's the other penthouse across the hall."

Ivy blinked a few times. Jordan thought she was about to hand him back the keys. Instead, she swallowed hard, put the keys in her jean pocket and gathered her bags. He watched her pack the rest of her things and pile them by the door. He tried to help, but she refused any assistance from him. No words passed between them but the tension in the air was stifling.

Finally, Ivy opened the door and looked back at him. "Thank you." Putting everything on the other side of the door, she looked at Jordan. The sadness in her eyes made his chest tighten. He wondered if this hurt her as much as it was hurting him.

The sounds of the door shutting and connecting with the locks felt as if the door of his heart had also been slammed shut. What was he supposed to do without Ivy?

Twenty-Five

"Are you ready?" Ivy asked Zoe.

"I've *been* ready. I got up super early, worked out, ate, and now I'm here sitting on my thumbs waiting for you. I'm so excited I don't know what to do with myself. I already spoke to my mom twice and your mom once. Ethan and the baby probably won't answer any more of my calls." Zoe cackled.

"Okay. I'm on my way to get you now." Ivy was so happy to see Zoe. It would be several weeks before she got to see any other family members. She grabbed her purse and headed to the door. "And I can't wait until dinner. You're going to love this place."

Ivy stepped out the door at the same time Jordan walked out of his. Her heart skipped. A few awkward seconds passed.

"Hey, Zoe. Hold on one sec," Ivy said and muted her phone.

"Good morning," Jordan said. His usual bright smile appeared dull.

"Morning," Ivy said and spread her lips into a cordial smile.

Another few seconds passed. Jordan wasn't apologetic at all about his desire for Ivy. She could see it in his eyes. No matter what, she needed to keep her distance.

"Have a good shoot today. I may stop by."

"Thanks," Ivy said.

More seconds ticked by. "Okay. See you later." Jordan walked to the elevator.

"I'm back," Ivy said, taking the other woman off mute. She continued chatting with Zoe but waited for Jordan to get on the elevator before walking down the hall and pressing the call button herself. "I'm getting on the elevator. I might lose you. I'll see you in a few." She ended their call.

Downstairs, she headed to the car that waited on her. Despite keeping his distance, Jordan made sure she had a ride to work every day even if he no longer rode with her. The time alone gave her the space to think.

Ivy's days on the set had grown increasingly awkward since she left Jordan's penthouse. When he was around, she spent all of her energy trying to act like his presence didn't affect her. On the days he wasn't there, Ivy longed to see him. At the penthouse, listening to him come and go sent her mind wandering. Who was he spending his time with? How long would he be gone? When would he get back? Less than a week had passed but it felt like she'd been missing Jordan forever.

Ivy made the right choice. Didn't she? She couldn't tell Jordan that she needed to leave because she was falling for him harder and faster than she could have ever imagined. Her feelings for him started to affect everything. She found herself acting out of character, getting jealous when other women were around him on the set, losing her focus. Ivy loved being the Money Maven, but behind the scenes, she valued her privacy. Those gossip posts about her and Jordan really upset her and she didn't want them to negatively impact either of their careers.

Getting out of his house and separating herself from him was supposed to help her figure things out. It didn't work. Being away from Jordan was hard to bear. Ivy thought about him constantly. She missed him terribly.

Dale's visit to the set that week went extremely well. She was elated about being at the studio, and squealed in delight when they asked her to join Ivy in one of the scenes at a local restaurant. After spending time with Ivy both on and off the set, Dale told her that she understood Ivy's mission to help women become financially savvy. She'd added that Ivy's goal went beyond telling women what to do what money; she helped women understand the importance of building a legacy of wealth. It was empowering. And despite some of the ridiculous antics of the celebrity clients she worked with on the show, this came through.

When Dale returned to New York, she told Ivy that she was looking forward to transferring her assets to Blackwell. That fifty-million-dollar portfolio would be the largest of all her women customers. Bill was ecstatic. Ivy invited Dale to come back to LA with her family for the show's upcoming wrap party.

Ivy was so glad that it all went well. She'd never worked so hard to close a deal with a client before in her life. When Dale left to go back to New York there was nothing to distract Ivy from missing Jordan. Now Zoe had arrived and would help to keep Ivy's mind off him—at least for the two days that she would be there. Zoe needed a break and Ivy encouraged her to come for a visit. Only, Zoe stayed at a hotel. She didn't want to invite her to the penthouse. She never would have been able to hide all the tension between her and Jordan in such close proximity.

The driver pulled up to Zoe's hotel. Ivy dialed her and let her know she was downstairs. Minutes later, Zoe came bursting through front entrance of the hotel. Ivy jumped out of the car and met her with open arms. The two hugged, swaying like long-lost friends who hadn't seen each other in years. It had only been weeks and they usually spoke daily.

"I'm so happy to see you!" Ivy gushed to Zoe as they slid into the car.

"I'm glad to see you too. And I can't wait to see you in action. I still can't believe you have a show. Ethan told me to take plenty of pictures."

At the studio, Ivy gave her a tour of her trailer. Zoe took a selfie next to her name on the outside. Ivy went to wardrobe and makeup, came out and modeled for Zoe.

"OMG! You look amazing!"

"Ha! It's like playing dress-up every day. It's crazy."

One of the production assistants told Ivy they were ready for her to shoot her wrap-up from the day before.

It took a few takes, but Ivy was able to get through it without stumbling over her words. She was getting better at this part every day.

Through her peripheral, Ivy caught a glimpse of Jordan. She didn't have to see him fully to know it was him. Her body responded to his presence before she ever set eyes on him. Butterflies would take flight in her stomach if she heard his voice or witnessed his sexy gait. She stiffened just a little. She looked for Zoe, who had walked to the other side of the set. Ivy was glad her sister-in-law wasn't there to witness her body's response to Jordan's arrival. Zoe noticed nuances like that all the time.

Ivy pushed through for the rest of the day. Once they let her go, she couldn't wait to leave the set.

"Dinnertime!" she announced to Zoe, trying to sound cheerful.

"Great! I'm starving and that food they have over there is a bit too fancy to get me full."

"Good evening. You must be Zoe?" The sound of Jordan's voice made Ivy's heart pause. "Ivy." He nodded and turned his attention back to Zoe.

"Yes, and I believe you're Jordan Chambers."

"I am. It's great to have you here. I hope you're enjoying your trip so far. Ivy is amazing in front of the camera, isn't she?"

Jordan's glance made air swirl in Ivy's chest. Why did he have to be so handsome, even when he was being dry and cordial?

"Yes, she was. I'm so proud of her."

"Me too. I think this show is going to be a hit with the viewers."

"Oh, for sure! It's got everything. Glitz, glam, spoiled celebrity brats with ridiculously bad financial habits and some heartfelt lessons. Plus, my sister here is absolutely beautiful. We know TV land loves a pretty face."

"I have to agree with you on all those points—especially that last one," Jordan said, glancing at Ivy.

Her cheeks warmed. "Thanks." Ivy smiled. "Well, we have some really exciting dinner plans…" She grabbed her bag.

"Sure. Don't let me stand in the way of a great meal." His eyes lingered on her face for a moment. "Have a good evening, Ivy." He turned to Zoe. "It was nice meeting you. Enjoy your stay."

"That man is a work of freaking art!" Zoe said once Jordan was out of earshot. "I thought things were going well between you two. Did I sense some tension?"

Ivy sighed. "I'll tell you over dinner." She texted the driver. "Let's go." She and Zoe headed out of the hotel and jumped in the car the moment her driver arrived.

Within fifteen minutes, they arrived at the Mexican restaurant Ivy had grown to love since she'd been in Los Angeles.

"Before you order, let me tell you all about my favorites," Ivy said once they were seated.

"All of it sounds delicious. Let's order different meals and share."

"Perfect idea." Ivy waved over their server and they put in their orders.

"Now, what's up with you and that gorgeous man?"

She told her sister-in-law everything. When she was done speaking, she expected Zoe to agree with her side and offer her some moral support. When Zoe didn't speak right away, she furrowed her brow and stared at her.

"What is it? Just spit it out already," she demanded, growing uncomfortable under Zoe's narrowed gaze.

"Are you kidding me? You're walking away from this man, who has been nothing short of amazing, because you can't control your hormones?"

"Zoe!" Ivy looked around to see if anyone else in the restaurant had heard her. "You're oversimplifying this as usual."

"Okay. Maybe I am, but listen to yourself and admit the man was right. You can't control people—especially social media trolls. Who cares if you fell into his bed before, after or during the production of this show? You are two grown, consenting adults. As long as you weren't taken advantage of, you have the right to do whatever you wish. Do you like him?"

"I…" Ivy huffed, buying time.

"Yes! You do. It's written all over your face. So, if you like him, screw what anyone else has to say and go for it." Zoe sat back. "You've been out of the dating game for so long you forgot how to play."

"Zoe, he lives clear across the country."

"So what! And he has an apartment in Manhattan. Somehow the two of you have found a way to consistently see each other until now."

Ivy lifted her chin. "Once the show is over, that will change."

"Does he have a girlfriend, fiancée, wife?"

"No."

"Neither do you," Zoe reminded her. "So, what's stopping you from being with Jordan?"

Ivy groaned, and fluffed her full hair. "I really don't have the time to nurture a relationship right now. I've been offered a second book by my publisher. And this show will air soon. That's going to lead to more engagements and Dad is only temporarily happy because of this big win from Dale." She blew out a breath. "My schedule is filling up by the minute. And in all honesty, I don't know how much longer I'll be able to stay at Blackwell. I may need to go part-time or stay on in name only to help you out with the women's initiative. You know that." Ivy sat back hard.

"And all of that means you can't date? I'm confused."

"*What?* I'm not saying that."

Zoe folded her arms, making her statement. Ivy looked at her and rolled her eyes. "Ivy, none of that means that you have to walk away from a man that you obviously care about. Stop making excuses. I know you want to be with this man, so be with him. You don't owe anyone any explanations but you do owe it to yourself to be happy, and if being with Jordan makes you happy, go get your man even if it scares you to pieces!"

Zoe had summed it all up. But the truth was, Ivy *was* scared. She'd messed up so many relationships before. What if she messed this up with Jordan too?

Twenty-Six

Jordan's day started out well but quickly went sour. Running into Ivy on and off the set had become taxing. As much as he wanted to pull her aside and kiss her breathless, he had to keep his distance. He gave her the space she needed and hoped that things would come together after their shooting schedule was over. Once the show went into postproduction, she'd head back to New York and Jordan could figure out his next step. As for now, seeing her without being able to take her into his arms was like torture.

He'd stopped by the set to check in with the crew. When he laid eyes on Ivy, the tempo of his pulse increased. Jordan started from her feet and slowly swept his gaze upward. Sexy pumps gave her foot the perfect lift. An off-white pantsuit bestowed her with an air of elegance, yet didn't hide a single luscious curve, and the tapered jacket accentuated her waist. The silk blouse underneath was unbuttoned just enough to make his mind wander, her red kissable lips were edgy and seductive, and Ivy's beautiful full head of crinkly curls was pulled stylishly to one side. Plus, the makeup was *flawless*. She looked hot and all business at the same time.

Ivy stood next to one of the celebrities from the show but completely outshined them. Jordan knew she was right about one thing. It was easier for him to focus at work when she wasn't around. He could never seem to keep his eyes off her.

She glanced up. Jordan and her locked eyes. Longing shot through him like a lightning bolt. She blinked and her lashes fluttered. She was absolutely exquisite. Anderson had to call his name twice before his voice registered in Jordan's ear.

Tearing himself away from that perfect vision, Jordan headed to over to Anderson to discuss scheduling. Then his phone rang. His stepfather's number came up. Jordan looked at the number, felt the phone vibrate and contemplated whether or not he should let it go to voice mail. Their last exchange wasn't good. Tim said some pretty sharp words the last time Jordan was in New York. Jordan finally answered. Tim asked for him to call him back later that evening so they could talk.

Jordan ended the call wondering what the man had to say this time. He assumed he'd get a call from his mother by the time Tim called him back. She was still upset about how things went when her husband blew up.

Next, Jordan heard a scream followed by a huge commotion. Two of the contestants got into a fight and knocked over a bookshelf. Ivy fell trying to avoid getting toppled by the shelf and ended up twisting her ankle. Jordan helped her up and tended to her before addressing the incident.

For the next few hours, he and the crew spent their energy on settling the disagreement between the two spoiled-rich contestants and dealing with the damage from their altercation. One threatened to sue everyone on set until Jordan reminded him that he could be found in violation of his contract. Money wasn't the issue. The contestants could buy the whole studio. It was the fame they desired. They weren't well-known actors themselves. They were the grown children of entertainers and celebrities who relished getting fifteen minutes in the spotlight whenever possible. Jordan told him that this wasn't that kind of reality show.

By the time he got home, it was too late to call his stepfather back. Entering his penthouse, Jordan tossed his car keys on the marble-topped table near the door, headed straight to his wine cabinet and poured half a glass of scotch. He was mentally and physically drained. Flopping down on the couch, he sat in darkness. Only the light of the full moon illuminated the room. Jordan wondered if that moon had anything to do with the odd happenings of the day—the call from Timothy and the fight on the set.

Jordan sipped and rested his head against the back of the couch. He thought about his conversation with his stepfather. They would have to work something out for the sake of his mother. Tim was most likely asleep, but with the tension that resided between them, Jordan took his chances and called Tim back.

"I was waiting up. Thought you weren't going to call," the older man said.

"I just got in. What's up, Tim?"

"I wanted to apologize and talk to you. Last week my doctor thought my cancer had returned. After running tests, it hadn't. But that got me thinking. Life is fragile and I wanted to make things right with you boys."

"I'm glad you're okay."

"I never had kids," Tim said.

Jordan wondered where Tim was going with his statement. It seemed random.

"But I loved your mother from the first day I met her. I could see the pain in her eyes. I could *feel* it. And I wanted to make her happy. I knew nothing about raising kids, let alone teenage boys. I tried. But I couldn't break through your and your brother's grief."

Tim fell silent for a few moments. "Maybe I should have tried harder." He huffed. "Asking you boys for help was hard. My pride got the best of me. Honestly, I would never think that you guys would try to take advantage of me. And with my health challenges, your proposal makes sense. As I said, I realize how fragile life is. And though I know you boys will always be there for your mother, I want to do my part to make sure she's well taken care of if something happens to me." There was a long pause. "So, I'm signing the proposal and wanted to make sure you and Dorian were still interested in doing business with me."

"Wow!" Jordan was taken aback by Tim's admission. "We didn't make it very easy on you, did we?"

"You guys were young," Tim acknowledged. "I get why you resisted letting me into your life."

"We didn't know what to do with you when you came around. We just wanted our dad. I guess all of us could have done more to make things work better," Jordan admitted.

Silence expanded between them. After a while, Tim said, "If you'll have me, I'd love to do business with you guys."

"I'm okay with that. I'll reach out to Dorian. How about we review the terms together one more time and make sure we're all okay with everything. I'll be out there in a few weeks after this show wraps and we can tie up all the loose ends then. Deal?"

"Deal!" Tim said. After another long pause, Tim said, "Thanks."

They ended the call and Jordan placed his phone beside him on the couch. He rested his head against the back of the couch again. Moments later, there was a soft knock at his door. *"What now,"* he grumbled aloud. He just wanted to rest.

Jordan didn't feel like answering and thought about staying put right on the couch. The knock came again. He heard a voice call his name.

"Jordan." Ivy's sultry voice was muffled through the door but he knew it was her by the way his body responded with a tightening in his core.

Jordan sat up. He put his drink on the coffee table. He wondered what Ivy could want at this time of night and then remembered her ankle. Maybe she needed something. Was she in pain? Jordan shot up and headed to the door.

"Coming." He looked through the peephole to confirm. It was Ivy. She was gorgeous as usual. Clicking the locks, Jordan opened the door. He took a breath. She was no longer wearing the sexy white suit, but she looked just as alluring in her leggings and sweatshirt.

"Hi," Ivy said softly.

"Hi," Jordan murmured. He noticed she didn't move. "Want to come in?"

"Sure."

Jordan stepped aside to let Ivy pass. "I'm sorry. I meant to call and check on you. How's your ankle? Do you need anything?"

"It's fine. That's part of the reason I'm here. I wanted to thank you for helping me earlier. I can't believe what happened."

"Oh. No problem. Of course."

Ivy wrung her hands. Both stood awkwardly by the door. Several moments of silence wavered between them.

Jordan averted his eyes from her face. He couldn't stand to look at her lips. Because it just made him want to pull her into his arms and feast on her. He sighed. Ivy was in his system. She affected him. Despite the short amount of time, they had known one another, those words he'd almost uttered were true. He loved Ivy. He knew it then, but really knew it now after having to live without her. Jordan went to bed at night wishing she was beside him. He woke up reaching for her only to find the bed empty. It pained him to see her on the set, in meetings, in the building or around the neighborhood and not be with her, holding her hand or lying beside her. Jordan had incredible dates planned that they never had the opportunity to go on.

However, Ivy had to want him too. He'd always heard

a saying about letting things you love go. If it was meant to be she'd come back. He understood her position and was willing to wait until the show was out of the way. He hoped she'd still be interested in finishing what they started or at least seeing where things would go from there.

It had been years since a woman had a grip on Jordan's heart like Ivy had. He'd wait on her if he had to.

"Was there something else?" Jordan asked stiffly.

"Pardon?"

"You said you stopped by to thank me. Was there something else you wanted to say?"

"Yes." Ivy tilted her head. "Jordan, I'm sorry." She shook her head.

Realizing he still hadn't shut the door, Jordan closed it, turned and gave Ivy his full attention. "Sorry for what?"

Ivy looked to the ceiling, shut her eyes and sighed. Then she looked directly into Jordan's eyes. "For acting crazy. I was scared. You were right about everything. I didn't expect things between us to...ugh... This social media life, books, television, the trolls... This is all new to me. I know finance. It's pretty calm in this industry. What I'm trying to say is that... Jordan..." She called his name with urgency.

"Yes, Ivy?"

Her mouth opened but nothing came out. She closed it and tried again. "I miss you." Her voice was low.

"You..."

"I. Miss. You," Ivy pronounced louder. "It's been so hard staying this close to you and not being able to be with you. I don't know what you did to me!"

"Whatever it was, I think you did the same to me. I haven't stopped thinking about you."

"Really?" Ivy looked as if she would cry.

"Really. I've missed you too." Jordan took a step closer to her.

"Do you forgive me?" Ivy moved closer to him, lessening the space between them.

"No need to forgive you. I understand you."

Jordan didn't know what it was about what he said, but Ivy pulled him into her, held his face in her hands and kissed him. Overcome with emotion, Jordan lifted her into his arms, then placed her gently back on her feet. They kissed as if their lips were water in a dry desert. Jordan's heart beat hard in his chest as if it were just coming back to life. Ivy squeezed him tightly. They kissed until they ran out of breath.

Ivy looked into Jordan's eyes again. No words passed between them for several moments, yet he believed she understood what was in his heart and mind.

"I don't want to be with you just until the wheels fall off. I don't want casual sex or to just have some fun. I want you, Ivy. All of you. I want you to be my lady."

"I've never perfected this girlfriend thing but if you'll have me…" Ivy admitted softly.

"I don't expect perfection from you. We can figure this out together."

"There's so much to figure out," Ivy said, then threw her head back and giggled.

"So, let's have fun figuring it out." Jordan laughed too.

They kissed again. Long, lovingly and hungrily. Jordan finally tore himself away from her and smiled. She traced a finger along his chest.

"So. We're a…thing?"

"As long as you don't get mad if someone posts a picture of us on social media with a caption that says I'm your boyfriend," he teased.

Ivy playfully slapped his chest. "Silly. It will take some getting used to but I'm willing to deal with it." Ivy winked, eliciting a chuckle from him.

His expression changed abruptly when a thought came to mind. "Go get dressed. Put on something nice." He ushered Ivy to the door.

"For what? Where are we going?"

"On the date we were supposed to go on when you left."

"Seriously?"

"Yes. Put on something pretty and meet me back here in an hour."

Ivy took Jordan's wrist in her hand and looked at her watch. "It's late."

"A half hour. We still have time. Hurry."

Ivy scrunched her brow. "If you say so. Be right back."

In exactly a half hour, Jordan knocked on Ivy's door dressed in slacks and a stylish printed button-down shirt. She opened the door and all the air left Jordan's body. In that short amount of time, Ivy transformed into a stunning vision of sexiness. Her little black dress stopped midthigh revealing beautiful toned legs. Her hair, though perfectly styled, looked wilder and hotter than ever. Unable to help himself, Jordan pulled her in for a kiss.

"Let's go." Jordan grabbed Ivy's hand and led her laughing down the hall.

Twenty minutes later they were dining solo on a rooftop with a breathtaking view of downtown Los Angeles, while a world-renowned chef served them lobster, chateaubriand and sautéed veggies. Next, he took her to an exclusive club owned by an A-list entertainer. The average person had no idea places like this existed. Only the "who's who" of Hollywood and the entertainment scene were allowed inside.

Jordan and Ivy enjoyed the band and sang the lyrics from popular songs along with the crowd. Afterward they walked along the beach, hand in hand, as the moonlight rippled along the water. Ivy held her shoes in her hand.

"Ready to go home?" Jordan asked as they embraced under the moonlight.

"Home?" Ivy teased.

"Yes. My home."

"Why? You're tired?" she asked with a salacious smile.

Jordan gave her a seductive wink. "Not at all."

"Then let's go!" Ivy giggled all the way back to the car.

They started kissing in the elevator. His hands touched her everywhere. Ivy slid her hands under his shirt and caressed his skin. Jordan body grew hot and his erection strained against his pants. They kissed and laughed and kissed some more.

At the door, Jordan fumbled with the keys. Finally getting them in the lock, he swung the door open. Their lips connected again. Jordan kicked the door closed with his foot and locked it. They kissed their way to his room.

Ivy slid the arms of her little black dress down and

shimmied out of it. Jordan tossed off his shirt and pants. When they were fully naked, he pulled her to him and lifted her. Ivy wrapped her legs around his waist. Backing her up to the wall, Jordan entered Ivy. She moaned in ecstasy. Jordan's thrusts were full. Every stroke was intentional. Ivy scratched at his back, urging him to go deeper. He did. Soon after, his legs grew weak. He stood strong, keeping his stride until Ivy started to shiver. She whimpered, held him tighter and cried out when her climax claimed her. Jordan's release came immediately after. He grunted with each thrust until he felt life flowing through him. Then he pulled out. Ivy massaged the flow from his erection while Jordan bucked, holding the wall to keep from crumpling to the floor.

Afterward, Jordan carried her to the bed. Ivy snuggled in his arms as they talked about nothing and everything. Then they kissed until their bodies were set ablaze all over again by one another's touch. As Jordan entered her for the second time that night, he looked straight into her eyes. They didn't hold back this time.

"I love you, Ivy."

"I love you too, Jordan."

Twenty-Seven

"We're here!" Ivy announced and jumped out of the party bus, careful not to rip her formfitting dress. She waved her family out. It was important to her that they traveled to the wrap party together.

"This is so exciting!" Phoenix said, exiting the party bus that Ivy rented.

"I can't wait for you all to meet the cast and crew." she replied. "And I'm so glad you were able to join us," she said, turning to Dale as the woman cautiously stepped out of the bus.

"I wouldn't have missed it for the world," Dale said.

One by one, her parents, siblings and sisters-in-law pooled onto the sidewalk.

Standing tall, Bill looked around—a big grin on his face. His smile made Ivy smile. It wasn't often that Bill showed how proud he was of his children.

"When do we get to meet the dude?" her brother Carter teased.

His wife, Phoenix, swatted him playfully. "Leave her alone."

"Yeah. That's what I want to know," the oldest brother, Lincoln, said.

"Me too," Ethan echoed. "Zoe has already met him. So, I know he must be kind of normal."

"Really, Ethan?" Ivy gave him a sideways glance.

"Yeah. He's dating you, right? That begs a few questions." Ethan laughed. Ivy's brothers Carter and Lincoln joined in. Lydia shook her head.

"Grow up!" Ivy rolled her eyes and laughed.

"Okay. Let's get this party started!" Zoe raised one hand in the air.

Ivy led her family into the chic office building, up the elevator and to the top floor. The wrap party was being held at a penthouse venue with a rooftop that boasted stunning views of Los Angeles.

Ivy checked in at the table separating the venue from the private party room that cost twenty-five thousand dollars to secure. A red carpet led the path to where the festivities would be held. Cameras flashed nonstop as photographers snapped countless pictures of Ivy with her family. They took several pictures before changing up their poses. Bill and Lydia with Ivy. Ivy with her sisters and then her brothers. They made funny faces.

"Ivy!" Her assistant from her branding agency called her name. "Want me to take some photos of you with your family?"

Ivy paused for a moment. She tried not to mix her

public life with her family life. She thought a moment longer. "Yes. Take a few, please." Ivy pulled her family back together while her assistant took a few more shots.

"Hey, Ivy!" Someone else called her name.

"Hi, Nadia." After saying hello, Ivy introduced the daughter of one of Hollywood's biggest directors to her family.

A chorus of "Nice to meet you" was exchanged between Nadia and Ivy's family.

The door opened to the rooftop and Ivy turned around. She was hoping it was Jordan. It was Tyson and Kendall. She ran to them, hugged and kissed them both. They joined the rest of the family. Tyson kissed his aunt and uncle before loudly greeting his cousins. The women circled around one another, admiring each other's stylish outfits.

The door opened again. Ivy's eyes went straight to it. It wasn't Jordan. The longer she waited for him, the more anxious she became. Wringing her hands, she fought a mix of nervousness and excitement. Jordan was going to meet the rest of her family. How would Bill and Lydia respond? She wasn't really worried about her brothers. They were mostly bark.

Several other reporters called Ivy. She excused herself from her family, leaving them to get comfortable and enjoy themselves. She smiled for pictures, took selfies and mingled with the crew and cast as they arrived.

Despite being anxious, Ivy sighed. She looked around the wrap party and realized how far she'd come in the past few months. The women's initiative at Blackwell was wildly successful and had grown even more once

Dale signed and started sharing with her network of very wealthy woman. Ivy's book made the *New York Times* bestseller list. She was the star of a reality show. It was a lot to take in but she was working at becoming more comfortable with her newfound fame every day. Even the social media trolls didn't bother her the way they used to. She'd done it. She made a name for herself outside of being a Blackwell. The best part about all of this was the most unexpected—she'd found love.

A hand slid around her waist from the back. Without turning around, she knew exactly who it was. Ivy knew his scent. She could feel his presence. Immediately she'd relax whenever he was around. Ivy finally turned around and put her arms around Jordan's neck. He kissed her lips. It was a peck but he'd done it slow and sweet.

"This is your night," he said, holding the small of her back.

"It's your night too."

"Okay. It's *our* night. Are you okay?"

"Yes. I'm fine. I'm excited."

"Good. If you feel like you need to get out of here at some point and go put on some leggings and a hoodie, just give me a signal."

Ivy chuckled. "I'll be fine. Come meet my family."

"Oh, boy!" Jordan let Ivy lead her to them.

"Mom. Dad," Ivy called out as she moved across the room. She waved at her siblings. When they were all together, Ivy said, "This is the executive producer, Jordan Chambers."

"Hello, Jordan," Bill said and shook his hand.

"You must be Mr. Blackwell," Jordan murmured. "And this must be your lovely wife." Jordan nodded and shook Lydia's hand as well.

"Nice to meet you. So, you're that gentleman that's trying to make my baby girl a star." Tight-lipped. Lydia looked him up and down before finally releasing a smile.

"Oh, no, ma'am. She's a star all on her own."

"I'm glad you recognize that."

Jordan greeted Ivy's brothers and sisters.

"And!" Ivy said, getting everyone's attention. "FYI he's also my boyfriend."

"Mmm," Zoe moaned and burst out laughing. The other ladies joined her.

"I see…" Bill said.

"Well, now," Lydia murmured. "I guess dinner is in order so we can get to know you a little better. Tomorrow evening at a place of your choice?" She looked at Jordan as if she dared him to say no.

"Absolutely."

"Good answer!" Ethan said and everyone fell out laughing again. "This calls for another drink. What do you say, fellows?" The men agreed. Jordan walked to the bar with Ivy's brothers and cousin.

Jordan looked back and winked at Ivy, letting her know he was going to be fine.

Ivy breathed in and let out a long exhale. She was glad that this part was over. So far, they all seemed to embrace Jordan. That made her happy because he was her peace.

Someone clinked a glass, gathering the attention of everyone in the room. They welcomed everyone and called Jordan and Anderson to the center of the room. Anderson told everyone how they came to the idea of this show. His energy lit up the room. When they were done, everyone applauded. The music became louder and people filled the room dancing.

Jordan found his way over to Ivy. Somehow, they became the center of attention. A circle formed around them. The DJ put on the rap song they'd sung together in the shower. Ivy's eyes grew as wide as her smile. She looked at Jordan, daring him to sing with her.

"Somebody, give me a mic," he said.

Her assistant ran to the DJ and brought a mic back to her. In one hand she gathered the bottom of her shimmering dress. In the other, she held the mic to her mouth and started reciting the lyrics. Jordan pumped his fist in the air. The crowd around them became hyped, cheering her on as she sang. Ivy and Jordan sang the chorus together. She handed him the microphone and he performed the second verse.

While he sang, Ivy danced and swayed, pumping her fist and cheering him on. People were snapping pictures. She didn't care. Joy filled her heart, making her giddy. Jordan finished his verse. Ivy thought he was going to hand the microphone back to her. She reached for it but the artist who sang the song stepped into their circle and took over. Ivy froze. Her mouth dropped open. Her eyes were as wide as saucers. She covered her mouth and laughed as the rap artist D Murphy sang to her.

Ivy looked at Jordan and pointed to the guy as he performed. Ivy couldn't believe it. She was having the time of her life. D. Murphy waved her over. She joined him and Jordan, singing the rest of the lyrics with him. When they were done, everyone cheered. What a surprise! She hadn't expected him show up. Ivy thought they would all go back to dancing but that didn't happen.

"Ivy," D Murphy said her name. "I have a special message for you."

"For me?" Ivy reared her head back. She looked over at Jordan. He shrugged his shoulders. She looked at Anderson. He held both hands up as if to say he didn't know what was going on either. "For me?" she asked again.

"Yes. You see my man here—" he put his hands on Jordan's shoulders "—has a question for you."

Butterflies took flight in Ivy's stomach. "Wait! *What?*" Ivy looked around. No one else seemed surprised by any of this, not even her parents.

The artist proceeded to rap about her and Jordan's first encounter and then the second. Everyone laughed. Ivy blushed. The rest of his lyrics had her stunned. Tears flowed from her eyes. He sang about how she came into Jordan's life like a force and knocked him off his feet. Then she'd put him on ice. Everyone laughed. But then, when she agreed to come back to him, it made him the happiest man alive. He reached out to her family, got her father's and brothers' blessing and got interrogated.

Her brothers walked out onto the floor. Ethan took a ring box out of his pocket. He handed it to Carter, who handed it to Lincoln. Lincoln looked at Jordan and raised a brow. More laughter. He handed the box to Jordan, but pulled it back and wagged his finger at Jordan. Jordan gave him the thumbs-up and took the velvet box.

He opened it and dropped to one knee. Both hands flew to Ivy's mouth. Tears sprang in her eyes and she gasped for air. Ivy stood frozen in her shock. Phoenix, Zoe and Britney, who had made their way beside Ivy, nudged her forward.

D Murphy handed the microphone to Jordan.

"Ivy Blackwell. It doesn't take long to realize when you've got a good thing. You make me a better man. Now, I'd love if you'd make me the happiest man. Will you marry me?"

"Jordan! Yes. Yes, I'll marry you."

Jordan stood and Ivy wrapped her arms around his neck.

The room burst into applause. The DJ threw on another song by D Murphy. The crowd sang with him.

Despite the frenzy around them, Ivy and Jordan swayed in each other's arms as if a love song were playing instead of an up-tempo rap song.

"When did you contact my family?"

"The day after you said you loved me back."

"Wow!" she said breathlessly. "You sure didn't waste any time."

"Those days without you showed me how much I wanted to be with you. I was going to wait on you no matter how long it took, even though I was hoping you'd come around after the show wrapped. Thank goodness you came to your senses before that."

Giggles bubbled out of Ivy. "I'm glad too."

Jordan kissed her lips again "I could kiss you all night," he said.

"I can't get enough of you either," Ivy whispered.

"Good, because I plan to be around for a long, long time." Jordan pulled her in and kissed her like no one else was in the room.

* * * * *

HARLEQUIN
PLUS

Announcing a **BRAND-NEW** multimedia subscription service for romance fans like you!

Read, Watch and Play.

Experience the easiest way to get the romance content you crave.

Start your **FREE 7 DAY TRIAL** at
<u>www.harlequinplus.com/freetrial</u>.